Button Mashers

A NOVEL

KATELYN HOOK

For Jason, my forever duo partner.

Chapter One

JENNA

"That's it! Who is he? Who's Jenson?" Carter yelled.

I tugged my hat down farther and shoved my controller and headset into my bag, ignoring Carter's outburst.

"Come on, Jenson! Show yourself!" He clenched his fists as he scanned the bar, but no Jenson stepped up.

This was not the first time Carter made a scene after Jenson eliminated him in a tournament, but he was starting to get out of hand. It began as a joke to him, and he would laugh it off. But after continuously coming in second place, his call to finding Jenson became more serious.

Button Mashers, the arcade brewery, was packed for a Wednesday night. Tournament nights for the wildly popular game *Total Command* brought in competitors and spectators alike, either milling around the tournament action, where the game systems lined the walls, or drinking and playing the retro arcade games on the other side of the bar.

I blew out a breath once Carter's friends finally placated him with a beer and he abandoned his search. No one could help him, because no one in the room knew who the mysterious Jenson was.

I scanned the bar again, but everyone had moved on to drinks and the arcade games. I slung my bag over my shoulder to make my way to the restroom, when I locked eyes with a man standing off to the side by himself. I didn't see him initially, and I wondered why he was alone when everyone else was here with a group of friends. He sipped his beer and, for a second, I thought maybe he didn't see me. It was as if he were looking right through me.

I blinked.

My subtle movement must have brought him back to the present; his blue eyes flickered to life, and his brows furrowed briefly before he feigned indifference. My hand subconsciously flew up and touched the *Total Command* character mask covering most of my face. I averted my eyes and escaped into the back hallway.

Alone in the hall, I tested the handle to the ladies' room: unlocked. I slipped inside and locked the door behind me. The single-user restroom was perfect—I didn't need interruptions as I transformed.

I dropped my bag on the ground, kicked off my Vans, whipped off my mask, and then removed my oversize hoodie. My long brown hair fell around my shoulders. I climbed out of my green cargo pants and was left in my leggings and a camisole. Reaching into my bag, I grabbed my long sweater, pulled it on, and slipped into a pair of wedge booties.

To complete my metamorphosis, I turned to the mirror and applied a quick coat of mascara and some lipstick.

I studied my reflection. Gone was the shapeless body and plain face that blended in as just another guy in the tournament, and in its place was a woman. My hazel eyes popped from the makeup, and the sweater hugged me, revealing my curves. My disguise was flawless. The mystery would continue. No one would know that I was Jenson before stepping into this room.

Satisfied with my appearance, I shoved all my discarded clothes into my bag and threw open the door.

To my surprise, Mr. Blue Eyes was standing in the hall, looking around with a confused expression.

I stopped. "Excuse me. Are you looking for something?"

His head swung toward me, eyes widening when he met mine. But then they returned to that distant haze I saw earlier.

He shoved one hand in his pocket and ran the other through his hair.

"No. I mean, yes. I thought that guy Jenson went this way. I wanted to congratulate him."

I tore my eyes from his and stared at the floor.

"He always leaves out the back door." I turned toward the exit down the hall and pointed. "Doesn't try to stick around."

I glanced back at him and noticed he was studying me. His eyes wandered to my bag, and I pushed it behind me. My stomach flipped. I had never seen him before and wondered if he was one of Carter's friends seeking Jenson's identity. Panic gripped me. If he knew...

My mind raced, ready to make excuses or justify why I disguised myself. If my cover was blown, I would be the one with the last word.

Finally he nodded, accepting my answer. I took that as my cue to leave.

"If you'll excuse me." I brushed past him and darted toward the bar before he could ask any more questions.

Once I dropped my bag behind the bar—where Lewis, let me keep it—I plopped down on a barstool. Lewis slid me a rum and Coke.

"On the house," he said.

I took a long sip and smiled. "You know that's not necessary."

Lewis held up his hands in objection. "On the contrary, I always reward the victor with a drink on the house. My bar. My rules. Which reminds me..." He passed me the gift card I'd won.

I chuckled. "Kitty Cause Café?"

"Yup. They're sponsoring this week. Go have lunch and play with the kitties!" he teased. He knew I preferred dogs so a gift card to a cat café was not my first choice. It was a free lunch though.

I wrinkled my nose. "No thanks. I'll bring Alyssa and Bryan. Alyssa will love it."

Alyssa and Bryan were my best friends from college, and they were also dating. I met Alyssa freshman year when we were randomly assigned to a dorm room together. Her bubbly personality was contagious, and we became fast friends. I met Bryan in a computer programming class, and we worked on a lot of assignments together. Naturally, Alyssa and Bryan met through me. Their personalities could be a bit opposite at times, but it seemed to work.

Lewis shrugged. "Yes, Alyssa will love that. I heard Carter yell. Do you think he'll ever figure it out?"

"Nope. My disguise is too good." I furrowed my brows, remembering Mr. Blue Eyes in the hall, but brushed the thought away and refocused. "Carter could win. His problem is that he locks onto one idea of how to beat me and misses the bigger picture. That's why I was able to sneak up from behind and eliminate him. He didn't anticipate my next move."

Lewis slung the towel over his shoulder. "Keep competing like you are and he probably won't ever win."

Lewis was the only one in the bar who knew I was Jenson. It wasn't that long ago that I wandered in here while walking around downtown. I remembered his excitement as he pushed the flyer toward me.

"I'm starting my second annual gaming tournament for the brewery. It's going to be amazing. The streaming platform Simmerz is sponsoring. Winners could get into their SimmerzCon tournament."

My ears had perked up at the mention of SimmerzCon. That was the tournament that *he* had won and bragged about. A person I tried to forget. Would he be at SimmerzCon again?

A fire had started in my belly and I began to plan. I would make it to SimmerzCon. I would show him. I would show all of them what I could do.

A hand had waved in front of me. Lewis stood before me with his eyebrows raised.

I snatched the paper, folded it, and put it in my purse. "I'm in!"

Lewis high-fived me. I realized quickly I would need to trust someone, and something about Lewis told me that he was my guy.

"But Lewis? You can't tell anyone who I am."

Lewis's eyebrows pinched together. "What do you mean?"

"You'll see."

On the first tournament night, he did. He saw my disguise and just shook his head. But he never asked why. He just went along with it, and now we had a routine. I showed up, played the tournament as Jenson, transformed, and then collected my victory drink and gift card for whichever local business had donated for that night.

Now loud cheering from the arcade side drew my attention. Carter was leaning over a game with a cocky grin while his friends cheered him on. I rolled my eyes. It didn't matter that Carter was a talented gamer. The fact that he turned a loss into a personal vendetta gave me pause, making me keep my distance.

"Lewis!" a woman called.

Lewis strolled over to her and flashed her a smile. She twirled her hair and giggled at something he said while he prepared her drink. He passed her the drink and, in return, she passed him a slip of paper, which he pocketed. He walked back over to me.

"How many numbers do you have in there?" I asked, pointing to his jeans.

"First one tonight."

"You going to call her?" I looked over at the woman, who gave me the death glare. I ignored it. I figured any of the new women who came in and made a claim on Lewis assumed I was flirting too.

"Nope," Lewis replied, emphasizing the P with a popping noise. He frowned and got back to work, pulling glasses from the dishwasher.

Even I gave Lewis a second look when we first met. But we never made it past our initial flirtations. It soon became clear to me that while charming, he was very driven to make his brewery successful, and neither of us were looking for a relationship at the moment. We developed an easy friendship as I kept showing up to play games and he kept me laughing with the latest stories about customers.

When someone called Lewis over to make another drink, I took the opportunity to scan the bar again. The tournament side had regained momentum, with people starting up old N64 consoles to play *Mario Kart*. I felt a pang in my heart, as this game brought back cherished memories. It was an enjoyable multiplayer game to have in a social setting like the bar. At least four friends could gather around and race together, switching off if more than four wanted to participate.

I finished my drink and noticed a man across the bar staring at me: Mr. Blue Eyes. He had returned from the back hall and now, in the light, I could see more of his features. Messy blond hair stuck out of his beanie. With his arms resting on the bar top, his navy Henley was stretched over a muscular frame.

He sipped his beer and held up a finger to summon Lewis.

I narrowed my eyes as he said something to Lewis, who laughed, peeked back at me, rolled his eyes, and returned his attention to the man. Good—Lewis will tell this guy off and keep him away from me.

After a few more exchanged words, Lewis made another drink and set it down in front of me.

"What's this?" I asked, pointing to the drink like it was a foreign substance. Lewis knew I rarely drank and when I did, I kept it to one a night.

"That charming gentleman bought it for you. He insisted."

I glanced over Lewis's shoulder to the strikingly handsome Mr. Blue Eyes. The corner of his mouth turned up. It was the first semblance of a smile I'd seen from him. "Nuh-uh," I said to Lewis. "He was looking for Jenson after the tournament. Now he's ordering me a drink? It's too weird."

"Come on, Jenna. It's probably just a coincidence. Why don't you give this guy a shot? He's hot." Lewis waggled his eyebrows. I couldn't say I disagreed.

"You know why. I only have until May to compete. I must stay focused. I can't let anything get in the way. I can't risk another guy having a say in whether I am good enough to compete in gaming.

"Not everyone is going to be like that. I'm not like that." Lewis noticed my frown and softened his tone. "Jenna, you have to stop hiding at some point. Just be you."

I nodded but pushed the offered drink aside. I continued to sip my own, not wanting to argue with Lewis. He didn't understand. No one bothered me as Jenson. I was just another gamer among the masses. No one questioned if I belonged.

Across the bar, Mr. Blue Eyes was gone. Just as well. I sighed and swirled the straw in my rum and Coke, lost in thought.

"See, that face—it tells me everything I need to know. You do want to talk to him."

"We already spoke," I muttered.

Lewis's eyes widened. "Look alive," he said and dashed off to the other side of the bar.

The seat beside me squeaked as it was pulled out. The smell of pine and sandalwood captivated my senses.

"Enjoying your drink?" said Mr. Blue Eyes next to me.

"It's fine," I replied nonchalantly. I gestured toward the drink he bought me. "Thank you, but it wasn't necessary. I have my one drink for the night." I raised the glass in my hand.

"Is one drink your limit?"

"No. It's my preference. I don't drink much. Especially on nights when I'm—" I caught myself. "Not on weeknights. You can have the drink you bought."

He lifted his own glass. "I'll stick to my beer."

I shrugged. "It's your money."

His jaw clenched before he took another swig.

I shifted in my seat. Lewis was immersed in conversation with a woman, who touched his hand and laughed at something he said. I felt Mr. Blue Eyes watching me.

"I didn't properly introduce myself earlier," he said, drawing me back in. "I'm Eric."

"Dark hallways are generally not a great place to meet."

His mouth tilted up slightly. Was he surprised by my lack of interest? I finished my first drink and eyed the second. What could it hurt? I didn't want to let it go to waste. I pulled it toward me and took a long sip. A cough jetted out of my throat. Holy cannoli, what did Lewis do? Was he in cahoots with this guy?

I looked back over at Eric and took a few seconds to analyze him further, up close in the light. Beyond his ocean-blue eyes, a strong jawline, his face covered in stubble. I paused at his lips, the bottom one full and enticing. When he sipped his beer, I diverted my gaze then picked up my cocktail and took a big swig. A soft wave of heat rose from my neck. I couldn't tell if I was blushing or if the alcohol was hitting.

"What's your name?"

"Jenna. I haven't seen you here before."

"First time," Eric said. "I saw the ad for the tournament and thought I'd stop in to see what was going on."

"You're a gamer." I slumped my shoulders. Figures.

He scratched his chin. "No, I wouldn't say that. I mean, I like video games as much as any guy, but I don't want to compete. Those guys were impressive though."

I let out the breath I was holding. No matter how attractive he was, being a gamer was a deal-breaker for me. I couldn't go down that road again.

Then I froze. It hit me what he had said.

"Or girl," I corrected.

"Huh?"

"You like video games as much as any guy or *girl*. Gaming is not only a guy thing."

I shook my head. I grew up believing anyone—male or female—was capable of being a top-tier gamer. It wasn't until college, when my boyfriend at the time, Thomas, humiliated me by posting a video of me. I quickly broke up with him. But it stayed in the number-one slot on MyVid for three months, which means millions saw it.

Everywhere I went around campus, I noticed people whispering behind hands, laughing, shifting their eyes toward me. I kept my head down and got through the rest of college with Alyssa and Bryan at my side. When I graduated, I expected to go hunting for a job. But when Lewis presented SimmerzCon to me, I knew it was a way I could get back at Thomas. I postponed my career plans while focusing on gaming. In the meantime, I made ends meet by working at a coffee shop.

Thomas tried to ruin something that I loved. Something that shaped the memories I have with my brother as a child. I wasn't going to let that hang over me anymore.

For the first time that night, Eric smiled fully, taking my breath away. In that moment, he was all I could see.

"Or girl," he agreed. His eyes danced around my face, searching for something.

I cleared my throat and motioned to Lewis. He filled a cup of water and set it in front of me. I took a long drink.

"That being said, how about we play a classic?" He gestured toward the arcade. "And how about we make it interesting?" His eyes were filled with mischief, and I wondered what he had up his sleeve.

I bit my lip and thought for a moment. I doubted he knew I was Jenson, but honestly, I wasn't used to this kind of attention, plus he's a gamer, he's a gamer, he's a gamer. But my love of competition and curiosity won out.

I squinted, studying him. "How so?"

"What if the winner gets the loser's number?"

"What if the winner doesn't want the loser's number? Even if they took it, it's not to say the winner will call."

"Oh, the winner will call."

"Confident, are we?" I downed the rest of my water and slid off my stool, ready to compete. "Fine. *Space Invaders.* Three rounds."

Eric followed me to the game and watched over my shoulder as I clicked *Two Players.* This was not a side by side two player game, but one where you had to switch back and forth once the first player lost a life.

My ship popped up on screen, and I started shooting down the pixelated aliens. I mashed the shooter button and dodged missiles raining down on me, using the joystick to move back and forth. I could feel the warmth of Eric's body right behind me and my heart fluttered. I jolted the stick the wrong way, and a missile hit me.

Eric winked at me. "Do you want to give me your number now?"

I blushed, my body betraying me. I gritted my teeth. "No way. It's your turn."

He tapped *Start* as he stepped up to the machine.

In a moment of insanity, I quickly squeezed his bicep before stepping back. My face grew warm at the feel of the hard muscles beneath his Henley.

He whipped his head around to eye me. "Dang," he said, and jumped back into the game, barely avoiding a missile flying his way. "That was cheating!"

"I don't know what you're talking about. That second drink that *you* bought me must have thrown me off balance. I only grabbed your arm so I wouldn't fall."

"Liar."

It was just my poor attempt at flirting. I cringed inwardly. Flirting? What had come over me?

I worried he might break the machine with how hard he was

slamming the buttons. Luckily, these things were built at a time when durability was a key requirement.

"All right. Your turn," he said after his ship was hit.

He'd put up a good score so far, but I was determined to win. I defeated almost the whole fleet of aliens.

We switched again. It was impossible for him to catch up; I had already won with my score unless he pulled off a miracle. Another section of aliens came forward, and he shot at them. But then Eric jolted his joystick the wrong way and was struck. His ship flashed and then disappeared. He lost.

"Yes! I'm the victor!" I pumped my arms in the air and danced a jig.

Eric chuckled. He smiled as if he had won, and I realized I was making a fool of myself with my nerdy moves. Men I typically competed with didn't flirt with me. Then again, they didn't know I was a woman in disguise.

"That was impressive. You really know how to play." Eric's eyes sparkled as he continued grinning from ear to ear.

"This was easy compared to—" I slammed my mouth shut.

"Compared to... what?"

"Online gaming. Not that I play much. I mean, you should give it a try if you enjoyed the arcade version." I lowered my head and toed the ground. When I glanced back at Eric, his smile had disappeared, and he was looking toward the bar.

"It's okay," he said, shrugging. "As I said, I play a little bit, but I would rather be outdoors."

I breathed out a laugh. "A bit cold to be out now, isn't it?" February in Indiana had begun last week.

"No, it's perfect."

If he thought 30 degrees was perfect, he must be a bit unhinged. And that was an abnormal day this time of year; typically, it was colder. I glanced at the time and noticed it was getting late. I had the morning shift at the coffee shop tomorrow.

"Well, I need to get going. Thank you for the drink and the games," I said with a smile and grabbed my bag and coat from behind the bar.

Eric snapped out of his daze and followed me. "Wait, I owe you my number."

I paused. The realization of what I did hit me. I let my guard down. If only for a moment, for one game. To a guy who clearly believed video games was a guy thing. No. No *way*. What if he recognized me? He's probably seen Thomas's video. What if he was internally laughing? My mind yelled at me to run. So I did.

"It's okay." I shrugged and slipped on my coat. "I had fun tonight. It was nice to meet you."

"Jenna, wait." Eric stepped toward me, confusion in his eyes.

I rushed out the door, leaving him standing there before I could change my mind.

Chapter Two

ERIC

"Move in," I instructed my teammate.

We descended into enemy territory, our eyes peeled on the surrounding landscape.

"I think they're hiding behind the trees on the hillside," he said.

"I think you're right." The other team's position made things tricky, but it wasn't anything we couldn't overcome. "Cover me from the building. I'm going to push forward."

"Roger that."

I ascended the hill while my teammate took cover in a building below. He set himself up in a window where he could shoot, or drawback if needed. The other team must have spotted his movement because a flurry of gunfire came his way.

"E! On the right!" he shouted to me.

Up the hill, an enemy peeked out from behind a tree. I raised my gun, ready to fire, when the all-caps text on my other monitor caught my eye.

"WHO ARE YOU?"

"WHO ARE YOU?"

"WHO ARE YOU?"

The messages flew through my chat. Not this again.

I muted myself in the game and spoke to my moderator. "Drew, please take care of that." A moment later the messages were deleted, and the person was banned.

"Thank you," I muttered.

"E! What are you doing?" my teammate shouted.

He was shot out of the window with no way to recover unless

I got to him in time. The guy I intended to take out was gone. I descended back down the hill, running toward my teammate, but it was too late. They spotted me and finished off both of us. We lost the game.

"Thanks a lot, man," he said, sarcasm thick in his voice.

"Sorry, I—"

"Forget it. You're such a—" The game closed out of the match and brought me back to the lobby before my random teammate could say anything else.

I sighed and turned back to my other monitor and tried to read the messages that zoomed through my chat. Many were supportive while others were ragging on me. I looked up at my camera and forced a smile before remembering that it wasn't on.

"Man, that guy was upset." I laughed, finding it funny how angry people got over video games. It rarely bothered me though. I had already moved on. "Well, you can't win them all," I said into my microphone to my viewers. My voice reverberated a deeper inflection back into my headset. That's right—no camera and a voice-changer app gave me the freedom of anonymity while leaving my gameplay and personality intact, allowing me to entertain my audience. "I'll be back tomorrow evening. I'm going to change it up and try a new puzzle game. If I'm not feeling it, I'll play more *Total Command*."

I read some of the chat messages and answered questions. When I finally checked the time, it was already two in the morning.

"Thank you for all the love. Thank you for all the support." I then ended my stream with my trademark saying: "Remember chat, keep grinding."

I turned off all my equipment and sat back in my chair, running a hand down my face. After a ten-hour stream, exhaustion had set in. The metrics from the night told me I had the number of viewers I typically had.

This was Simmerz, a streaming platform where I played video

games. Viewers subscribed for a monthly fee and could get emotes and other perks, or they could donate money and include a note I would read online. It was my income, my job.

Unfortunately.

Not that I was ungrateful for what I did. Making a living playing video games every day was a dream. Only, it wasn't *my* dream. That was no longer a possibility.

I scanned the chat log of the viewer Drew had banned. I was fortunate to have Drew. He had watched my stream from the beginning and was helpful when I needed input, so I made him a moderator. He kept my chat under control, keeping it clean and friendly. The banned viewer had a history of spamming messages, which not only distracted me but irritated everyone.

My viewers only knew me by my gamertag, EHucker360, or EHucker for short. Some people called me E or Hucker. I responded to any of these names when gaming. When I started streaming two and a half years ago, I knew I had to grow quickly to make up to my family all that I'd lost, so I set goals for the community. This got my viewers involved and drove me to do everything I could to have a fun stream and a community that cared about one another.

One of those goals was to start using my face cam if I got to 6,000 subscribers on my channel. I set what I thought to be an impossible number since I never intended to reveal my identity. Except lately viewership had grown so much it was in the 4,000s. True, it's helped me financially, but if I wasn't careful, I'd reach that goal in a year or two.

Each stream made me equally excited and stressed. I *couldn't* show my viewers who I was.

I rose from my chair and stretched. The fresh night air called to me. I opened the door to my balcony and stepped out into the cold. I stood only in my T-shirt and shorts, barefoot on the frigid cement. I breathed in the crisp air, letting it fill my lungs. I tilted my head back to the dark sky, and feathery snowflakes melted on my eyelids and cheeks.

This. This is what soothed me; I found solace in the cold. It numbed my body, and it numbed my mind. I didn't have to *think*. I didn't have to *remember*. Ironically, the temperature I felt at home in, helped me to forget it.

The cold was how I ended up at Button Mashers last night. After my stream was over, I needed an escape—streaming had left me feeling caged in. Yet video games continued to find me. I went on a walk to clear my mind when I ran across the arcade brewery.

I had planned to have one drink and check out the tournament before heading home. Until I saw *her*.

She had sat in the farthest corner, wearing a baggy sweatshirt and a mask. I circled the room, checking out the different screens, until I stopped behind hers unnoticed. She was concentrating on securing a victory on a map I was very familiar with. I was mesmerized by her skill and determination, but I was also perplexed.

She blended in so well that I wasn't 100 percent sure until I saw her in the back hall. At first, I didn't believe she was Jenson, but then I saw her mask sticking out of her bag.

Why was she in disguise? Why was she hiding?

People didn't hide like me. People liked to show themselves off, to point at themselves and say, "Look at me, look at how great I am at this thing I do." She was exceptional. She had every right to smile and jump up in the air when she won, but she didn't. That drove me crazy with questions.

I fished my phone out of my pocket and opened the Simmerz app. I clicked the search bar and typed in *Jenson*. My heart pounded as one result popped up. I tapped on the profile, but it was blank except for the gamertag. So she didn't stream, but she at least had a Simmerz account. I wondered which streams she watched and if she ever watched mine. I had even more questions. She was involved in some serious competitive gaming. I itched to add her on Simmerz.

But I couldn't. Because of my recent growth in popularity, there was a good possibility she would have heard of me. And if she followed the game she competed in tonight, my stream would have been at the top of her suggested list, right after my friend Trekster's. It would be unexplainable if I randomly added her. She met Eric, the regular nongamer last night. Not EHucker.

I flexed my fingers and wiggled my toes. They were becoming numb. I could still move them though, so I had another two minutes or so.

I ran my hand through my hair. Took a deep breath. Tugged at a strand.

I didn't lie to her when I said I wasn't a gamer. It was my job. Those guys and Jenna *loved* what they were doing. There had to be a reason for her to mask her identity. I thought of the guy who made a scene after the tournament. Maybe that was why.

When I basically cornered her in the hall, I wanted to know everything. But seeing her as herself shocked me. I realized I couldn't just ask her.

A cold wind cut through me. Now I couldn't feel my toes. Not wanting to get frostbite, I pushed off the rail and walked back inside. Stepping into my bedroom, my ligaments burned as they regained their warmth.

It worked. I couldn't feel. I barely remembered except...

I pulled up my bank app and sent through my monthly transfer. Paying my penance. The only thing I could do.

I threw my phone aside and fell into bed. Sleep quickly found me.

The buzzing of my phone pulled me out of a dream.

"Gah, make it stop." Moaning, I rolled over to grab my phone, then glanced at the screen. "Hi, Mom." I yawned.

"Hey, sweetie. Were you still sleeping? What is it, eleven a.m.?"

Sighing, I sat up and rubbed my eyes. "Yeah. I streamed late. It's not a big deal. I don't have anywhere I need to be."

Mom huffed into the phone. "That's what I want to talk to you about. I got a bank alert on my phone. I told you we don't need—"

"Mom, I told you. I owe it to you and Dad. Take it and don't fight me on it."

"But—"

"Mom, please."

I got up and paced around my room. It was way too early for this conversation, so I refused to have it. They could have my extra money from streaming. It was my fault our family had to move to the Midwest.

"Eric, you need to search for a regular job. Something with normal hours, where you won't be sleeping all morning. You need to get back out there." Mom believed my streaming made me a recluse. It may have been partially true, but it was the nature of the job. I had a couple of online friends, and I was trying to meet people. It wasn't as easy as she made it seem. Mom was very social and was already heavily involved at church as well as two community groups.

"I went out last night to a bar. I met a couple of people. It was fun."

"Oh, good sweetie. I'm so glad to hear that. Are you still coming Sunday to pick up Emily?"

"Yup. I'll be there."

My seventeen-year-old sister and I had set up a monthly hangout. Even though we annoyed each other at times, we got along. Two years ago, with all of us settled in Indiana, I decided to move out on my own since I was already twenty-three. I told Emily we would stay close. This was my way to keep that promise.

Mom chattered on about Emily and her latest dance recital. Which I knew all about because I had snuck in and sat in the back row.

"Look, Mom, I've got to go."

"Okay, I'll see you Sunday."

I hung up the phone and hobbled into the bathroom. My knee was killing me today. After my shower, I would run through my stretches so I could function. I stripped off my shirt and stared at myself in the mirror. A tattoo of mountains around my bicep and a sun covering my shoulder masked the mess of scars left from my injury. The one over my right eyebrow was harder to hide. I had grown my hair out to cover it, but I knew it was there. I saw all of them.

If the pain in my knee wasn't enough to remind me of everything I lost, the scars were. I scowled, removed the rest of my clothes, and stepped into the shower. Turning the handle to *Cold*, the icy water poured over me. Like last night, the temp numbed both my body and mind. I tilted my head back and let the memories wash down the drain.

Chapter Three

JENNA

I prepared myself for the worst as I leaned on the door to the Kitty Cause Café. I stepped inside, preparing myself for the scent of "woman with nine cats," but instead I smelled... fresh bread? I looked around to find the place clean and inviting. Off to the side was a separate glass room, where people could play with the cats.

"Look at all the kitties!" said Alyssa, her face plastered to the window, watching the cats zooming around and playing. Bryan stood nearby, furiously typing on his phone. But when he saw me, he stuffed it in his pocket and stepped forward.

I smiled at my friend's excitement. "Come on. Let's eat before you play with the cats."

Alyssa pouted, and Bryan shook his head.

We placed our orders at the counter then found a booth. Alyssa slid in close to the wall, and Bryan sat beside her. I took the seat across from them.

"I can't believe a Kitty Cause Café gift card was your tournament prize this week and you invited us. I've been dying to come here since it opened," Alyssa gushed.

I laughed. "Now why would I bring anyone else, Alyssa? I knew you would freak out."

Bryan glanced at Alyssa, who bounced in her seat as she gazed toward the cat room. His eyes darted to mine. "Yeah. Thanks."

I smirked at him, and he stuck out his tongue.

"You're the best! Sometimes all that gaming you do is beneficial," she said.

"So glad you get to reap the benefits." I didn't mind. The gift cards and freebies were a bonus. I was after something bigger.

After a while, our names were called, and Bryan went up to the counter to get our food. Once he returned, we caught up on life while we dug into our sandwiches and salads.

"So obviously you won last night, but did anything else happen?" Alyssa asked. Besides Lewis, Bryan and Alyssa knew about my tournament disguise. They thought it was ridiculous, but they were also there during the worse of the viral video blowup.

"Well, Carter was on the hunt for Jenson again. I was worried he wouldn't let up this time, but thankfully his friends distracted him with a beer."

Alyssa rolled her eyes. "What's his deal anyway? Did he forget to learn humility in defeat?"

"I think Carter's world revolves only around him." I took a bite of my sandwich. "After I changed, I ran into a guy outside the restroom. He seemed confused. He was looking for me—well, for Jenson. I made up an excuse to escape to the bar."

"Interesting..." said Bryan.

"Then he bought me a drink." I stared down at my plate and a small smile crept up. When I glanced up, Alyssa was beaming at me; I hadn't talked about liking a guy since college.

"Eek!" Alyssa squealed. "Was he cute? Wait, you accepted? You never let guys buy you drinks."

"I wasn't planning on drinking it. Lewis set it in front of me and I didn't want to waste it. Did you hear me? He may have noticed me as Jenson!"

"You don't know that. Maybe he bought your excuse. I mean, I've seen your disguise, and there's no way he would think you were a woman."

"Hey."

Alyssa shrugged. "Anyway, what happened? Was he sexy?"

Bryan gave her the side-eye before taking a bite.

"He was handsome." I felt a rush of heat and eyed Bryan. He was downing his Reuben sandwich.

"You're blushing. Wait. How hot was he? Did you get his number?"

Bryan placed an arm around Alyssa to keep her from bursting out of her seat. "Lys, you're scaring her. Also, if you could put less emphasis on his looks, that would be great."

Alyssa pivoted in her seat and pecked Bryan on the cheek. "I'm only curious for Jenna. She deserves a hot man. Besides, you know how freaking sexy I think you are." She ran her hand down his arm seductively. Bryan gulped and stared into her eyes.

"Gross. Can you not do that now?" I fake gagged.

Bryan was more modest about PDA, but he couldn't resist Alyssa. She laughed and turned back to me. Bryan turned as red as I was moments ago.

"Fine, his name is Eric. I beat him at *Space Invaders,* and he claims he's not a gamer. I left without taking his number."

"You let him game with you?" Bryan asked, eyes almost magnified through his thick-framed glasses.

"Yes, it wasn't a big deal. We played three rounds, and that was it. I probably won't run into him again, and that's fine. Even if there was a spark, it would never work out anyway." I frowned at the salt shaker.

Alyssa elbowed Bryan.

"Ow. What was that for?" She made a face and nodded toward the bakery.

"Oh, I'm going to check out the dessert case. Be right back." Bryan got up awkwardly and made his way over to the bakery.

Alyssa raised an eyebrow. "There was a spark?"

"What are you talking about?"

"You just said there was."

"Oh right. Well, it doesn't matter. I figured..." I shrugged.

Alyssa placed a hand over mine and said gently, "Jenna, it's okay to be interested in someone again."

"Yeah, but I met him at Button Mashers. He already seemed suspicious about Jenson. What if he finds out I spend ninety percent of my time playing video games? What if he knows about the video? It's not worth going down that road again."

My mind flew back to a moment with Thomas, the moment when a certain uneasiness began.

The door was cracked open, and I had knocked lightly, but they didn't hear me over the gunfire of the game.

"Man, did you see that video of Lightning Lady?" Thomas said. "Her gameplay is trash, but she certainly looks good."

"I hear you. I mean her chest..." his friend said.

I pushed my way into the room. "Thomas, are we going to get dinner?" I tried to keep my voice even, pretending I hadn't heard. I knew of Lightening Lady, an amazing gamer. It was just guy talk, I told myself, even though no female gamer deserved to be spoken about like that.

Thomas sighed and passed the controller to his friend, then grabbed his coat. We left and started walking down the hall.

"Thomas?"

"Hmm?"

"Lightening Lady is a good gamer. Why would you call her gameplay trash?"

He stopped and leaned down to kiss me. I leaned into it, letting some of my frustration out.

"We were just joking, babe."

Alyssa waved a hand in front of my face, drawing me back to the present.

"Jenna, I know that look. You're putting him in the Thomas box already, before you even know him. You played a game with him, and he was still interested. Not all guys are going to turn out like Thomas. I mean take Bryan, for example." She gestured toward him studying the cupcakes like he was preparing for a culinary quiz.

I'd played games with Bryan before, but that was different. He was a close friend. I nodded like I agreed, but Alyssa was wrong. She didn't understand. Eric wanted my number when he thought I was just a cute girl at the bar. If he'd figured out I was Jenson, he wouldn't have given me the time of day.

I was right to run off.

I looked back at the counter. Bryan was now in line to pay. "So how are you two doing?"

Alyssa put her face into her hands. "Is he *ever* going to propose? I've been dropping hints and trying my best to have patience. It. Is. *Killing.* Me."

Chuckling at her agony, I told her, "You know he loves you. When he needs to, he shows up for you. Remember the night he rescued you from that party?"

In our junior year, Alyssa went to a party with a couple of our friends. I was out with Thomas, who didn't want to go. She was having a good time when some drunk guy tried to feel her up on the dance floor. Alyssa repeatedly told the guy no, and when he didn't listen, she locked herself inside a bedroom and texted Bryan.

Bryan came in a flash. A normally subdued man, Bryan yelled and cussed at the handsy man before taking her home, and he stayed with her until I came home. He returned in the morning with coffee and breakfast for both of us. It was at that moment Alyssa started seeing Bryan in a different light.

"You're right. I need to be patient." Alyssa sighed, resigned to a fate of waiting.

"Not easy for you, huh?"

She shook her head and laughed. "I think he wants to come back."

Bryan stood at the counter, holding two containers. When he saw us watching him, I waved him over, and he hesitantly approached.

"Everything all right?"

"Yes. We're great," Alyssa said, a bit curt.

I widened my eyes at her display of irritation, and she turned and smiled at me knowingly.

Bryan cocked his head and handed me a container with a strawberry cupcake. He held another box with their cupcakes in one hand and offered Alyssa the other hand. "Come on Lys, let's play with the cats."

Alyssa sprang from her seat. "Oh, good." She pulled me into a hug. "Thank you so much for lunch. Remember what I said."

"I will. You guys have fun."

Alyssa marched toward the cat room while Bryan trailed behind her, grasping her hand. I bundled up in my coat and gloves before heading outside to my car. I pushed the door open, and the bitter chill blasted my face.

Remembering Eric's affinity for the cold, I shook my head. Yup. Definitely unhinged.

Later that evening, I curled up on the couch under a blanket. I grabbed my Xbox controller and entered the Simmerz app. I pulled up TakeNote, a female streamer who was awesome at *Total Command,* and watched her for a half hour before she stopped and dropped us into a stream for a guy called EHucker360.

I sneered at the screen. I had heard of him because of his growing popularity, but I was not watching a guy play my favorite game. I started to change to a new channel when he caught my attention.

"TakeNote, thank you so much for dropping your community here," announced EHucker. "Chat, go check out TakeNote—she's an amazing streamer. A top-tier gamer on Simmerz. She's taught me so much about this game. I appreciate you so much, TakeNote."

At the top of his screen was a goal bar for subscribers, with the reward of him using his face cam.

My stomach dropped—his goal was substantial. It didn't seem like his chat would see his face anytime soon, or maybe ever.

"Oh shoot." EHucker was at the end of the game, with three players remaining. He ran in fearlessly and was able to take one person down. One player eliminated the other and then turned toward EHucker, who was ready and defeated the last player for the victory.

"Awesome! We won that, chat!"

Someone donated five subscriptions to the community, and an alert popped up.

"Thank you! Thank you for the subs. Who gets one? Marka, Snipes, Otterboy, Lance, and..."

EHucker cleared his throat. "And Jenson."

I typed a thank-you for the subscription.

"Jenson, a first-time chatter, welcome to the community. Okay, I'm going to play a couple more and then close out. Remember, we have some goals coming up. If I get thirty victories this month, we'll have a community night. At the end of the month, I'm gifting some in-game currency, Command Bucks, and as always there's oursubscribercamgoal."

EHucker rushed over the last words. I watched the chat scroll quickly, with several people cheering and pushing for subscriptions to reach the cam goal. Some were so insistent they shouted: *"SHOW YOUR FACE."* Those messages were quickly deleted by the mods.

I sat forward on the couch. I knew plenty of people who didn't use a camera to stream, and no one had this kind of push for a reveal.

I looked over at my bag that I'd thrown by the door. Inside were my oversize clothes and a mask from the other night. I could empathize with not wanting to share who you were with a bunch of strangers. But I wasn't always this way. I used to have confidence in myself. Now I was hiding in a corner, hoping to reach a goal I wasn't sure I could obtain.

Getting into SimmerzCon was not just a way to get back at Thomas. It was also something my older brother revered. He would spend hours gaming and competing in online tournaments with the aspiration of getting invited one day. I spent many hours watching him, and sometimes we even played together—some of the best memories of my childhood. One morning when I was thirteen, I woke up to find his room was empty. My brother had died after a drunk driver hit his car on the way home. He was only seventeen.

I blinked back tears and focused on the faceless streamer, a person who had set such a lofty goal as if to hide away forever. Then I picked up my controller and pressed *Follow.*

"Jenson! Thank you so much for the follow. Hope to see you back here next time. Okay, chat, I'm going to end it here. Remember, keep grinding."

I closed out of Simmerz and opened *Total Command* to start my first game and let my mind wander back to the other night at Button Mashers, and meeting Eric.

My gut told me he knew something. No one had ever gone searching for Jenson to congratulate him—me. I'll admit, there was an attraction there, but it was a one-time meeting. I was clearly possessed. I mean, first I played a game with him and then I squeezed his bicep. *Grrrr.* No, I was not myself. I should have just left. He wasn't a regular at the bar. I probably wouldn't see him again.

"It's fine," I told myself out loud. "Just fine."

I sighed. Nearing the end of my match, I found the last player, eliminated him, and won the game. Except this time, I didn't feel overcome with joy.

I felt alone.

Chapter Four

ERIC

When I got to Button Mashers Friday night, it had a different atmosphere than tournament night. Instead of competitive gamers concentrating on planned matches, the bar was bustling with college students drinking and facing off on every kind of game.

I snaked my way past a group playing an N64 multiplayer game and sat at the bar to wait as Lewis passed out the house beer he called Level Up. Two women grabbed their drinks from Lewis but stayed there, continuing their flirtations. Eventually, he nodded to his other customers and sent the women on their way.

"Hey man, welcome back," Lewis called out when he saw me. "What can I getcha?"

I ordered a beer on draft, and Lewis slid away to pour my drink. It was almost impossible to spot anyone with the number of people packed in. My attention beelined to a mess of black hair in the arcade: that punk from Wednesday night, looking smug as ever.

"Who is that?" I nodded toward the guy as Lewis set my beer in front of me.

He peeked over his shoulder and grimaced. "Carter. He's been coming here since I opened two years ago. He's a great gamer, but he can't stand to lose. And that happens a lot."

"To that Jenson guy?" It was clear Lewis and Jenna were good friends, and if anyone knew about the Jenson disguise, it would be him.

"Yeah. Mostly to... him." Lewis's eyes darted away from mine. "He was rather upset."

"You saw that? Man, I was this close to kicking him out. If his tantrums continue, I won't hesitate to show him the door."

I nodded and took a sip of my beer. The dude seriously had an issue with losing, and unfortunately for Jenson, it seemed like she was his only obstacle.

The door opened, and I swung my head around. A couple of people came in and ordered drinks from the other bartender. Lewis wiped a beer glass dry and grinned.

I arched an eyebrow. "What?"

"She comes in around eight on Fridays."

"Who?"

"Jenna. You know, the pretty woman with the brown hair you flirted with all night. I know you're not here for me."

He was right. I intended to find Jenna again even if it meant coming back to Button Mashers every single night—not that it was possible, as I had to stream. I hadn't decided yet on tonight. I considered doing a late-night stream. And Saturday—tomorrow—I had a sponsored stream, where a company paid me to play a game while promoting their product, and two viewers in my chat could win it in a giveaway. This time, it was a new gaming monitor.

I didn't exactly have a plan, but I wanted to know more about her. For once, I felt a warmth inside, and that was strange since I preferred the cold.

"Maybe I am here for you," I said, waggling my eyebrows.

He laughed. "Very funny."

"How long have you known her?"

"Just over half a year. She started coming here last July."

"Did you date her?"

"Me and Jenna? No. I mean, initially I flirted with her because I'm not blind. She's beautiful. But I'm so busy taking care of this place and she had other things on her plate, so our friendship just developed naturally. I don't really have time to date."

I relaxed in my seat. "So that slip of paper I saw you take from that woman the other night was what, a new recipe?"

"No. I threw it away later. Anyway, you must have something going for you. I'm surprised she talked to you."

"Why do you say that?"

"Let's just say she's probably not looking to date most guys who frequent this place. They're hardcore gamers. Guys have flirted with her and bought her drinks before, but she usually walks away or refuses. You're the first guy she didn't instantly reject."

"I'm not a gamer." For me, gaming was a means to an end, not who I was.

"Good. I suspect that's a deal-breaker for her."

My gut knotted. "Why?"

"That, my good man, I cannot tell you. I'm sure her best friends know, but I've only caught bits and pieces. Something happened in college is all I know." Lewis collected a few empty glasses sitting on the bar and started filling the dishwasher. "I like you, and I say go for it. But if you hurt her, I will not be happy." Lewis crossed his arms and held eye contact with me until I nodded in response.

He wandered off to serve other customers, and I observed people playing at the arcade machines. There seemed to be a good mix of men and women. I noticed two women facing off on *Street Fighter* while some guys cheered them on. I was still curious as to what triggered Jenna to disguise herself whether it be something that happened here or something else entirely.

I understood there was bias toward female streamers. I've seen things in TakeNote's chat that would never appear in mine. Of course, her mods quickly deleted the comments, but they were still said. On the flip side, there was a lot of positivity in gaming. It made me mad that Jenna wasn't experiencing that. I could show her myself except she'd met me, Eric, not EHucker.

A commotion from the arcade drew my attention. Carter was holding court with his group of friends. Well, I wasn't like that guy. My grip tightened around my glass. He would not be happy if he figured out who Jenson was.

"Lewis!" the other bartender called out. "All the kegs for tonight's special are empty."

Lewis checked the tap. "No way. They were on the list for morning crew to fill."

"I thought you were filling the kegs tonight."

Lewis took off to the back room, where the tanks were held. When he returned, he paced the bar. "The valve to the tank is broken. I can't access more."

"That beer is flying off the shelf tonight. What do we do?" the bartender asked.

With his jaw set, Lewis said, "Pull keg three out. Replace the special."

"Last week's beer? That didn't sell well."

"Discount it, twenty percent."

"We won't make margin."

Lewis clapped him on the shoulder. "I'll worry about that. You just concentrate on getting it in the tap and selling drinks."

Lewis walked up and down the bar for a moment before he focused on the task at hand.

"Everything okay?" I asked him.

"Not really. I messed up. I have to hold myself accountable. It'll knock me down for the month, so I'll have to shift some things around."

I glanced around the bar. "It looks like business is booming though. Everything'll work out."

"I hope. I put my heart, soul, and bank account into this place. If it fails, I fail. Then I've really proven them right."

"Who?"

Lewis waved me off. "It doesn't matter."

"That's why you don't have time to date?"

"It's not like I don't want to meet someone. But right now, I'm married to this business. But if the right woman came along, let's just say I'm not opposed." Lewis jutted his chin toward the door. "Speaking of meeting the right woman..."

A cool draft whooshed in and Jenna entered, sans disguise. She made a beeline for the game consoles but didn't hop on. She lingered a couple feet back from a woman who was playing, her eyes trained on the screen.

I sipped my drink and watched her for a few minutes. I itched to jump up from my seat, but my gut told me to wait. She was in the zone, standing with her arms folded and lips pursed in a straight line. Sometimes she would grin and sometimes she'd throw her head back in surprise.

"Yo, Eric. Before you wander off, put your number in." Lewis handed me his phone. I punched in my number and texted myself then handed his phone back. "Let's hang out sometime."

"Yeah, cool." Maybe I would call Lewis. I did need a reason to get out of my apartment and needed to make new friends. Streaming sixty-plus hours a week didn't leave time for much else.

I tucked my phone into my pocket. I glanced back at Jenna, who was still watching the gamer, but now Carter stood next to her, chatting. Every time he moved closer to her, she would step back.

Carter leaned in and tried to brush a strand of hair behind her ear, but she flinched.

I jumped to my feet. Nope. That wasn't going to happen again.

Chapter Five

JENNA

I bounced up and down on the balls of my feet as Sam eliminated player after player. It was only a matter of time before she secured a victory.

Button Mashers was busy, but I was here right now for one reason only: to be inspired by a genuinely good player and learn from her technique. Several people had gathered around Sam. She was a local gamer I liked following on social media. She wasn't a streamer or a competitor. She grew a following with clips and interactions on MyVid.

She was one of the best players in the game, and I admired not only how she played but how she handled herself online. She ignored the trolls and always pushed herself to make entertaining content. When I saw her post saying she'd be at Button Mashers, I had to come and watch. I no longer wanted to play at home today. Especially after what happened earlier tonight.

I had been enjoying myself playing *Total Command* with a squad and had my mic muted. Everything was going great, and I was about to join in on the voice commentary until things went sideways. Fast.

"Wayne, I saw you were gaming last night, so I watched for a bit. You were terrible. What happened?"

Wayne laughed. "That wasn't me, man. It was Melanie."

"She kept getting eliminated—immediately. Your girlfriend is hilarious."

"I know. I kept telling her to pick up better loot, but she wouldn't listen."

"Tell her to stick to *Animal Crossing* and *The Sims*."

"She's playing that now. Leave the men's game to the men. Hey, Jenson! Cover me, eh?" said Wayne.

Wayne was getting shot at as he crossed the open landscape for loot. Instead of helping, I exited the match. They reinforced my reasoning for not using a mic.

I released a breath now, shaking off the memory, and a heavy hand clapped onto my shoulder.

"Alone again?" Carter asked, his breath hot on the back of my neck.

I grimaced. I could leave, but I wanted to see the end of Sam's game. "No."

"Lewis doesn't count."

"What do you want, Carter?" I crossed my arms to give me some level of defense.

"I want to take you out."

I turned to face him. "I told you before, I'm not interested." I stepped back. Carter ignored my discomfort and moved in closer. I glanced back at Sam's screen. Her character was hopping onto the plane in the end-match victory credits. I scowled. I missed it.

"I don't get it," Carter said, bristling.

"What?" I asked before realizing I didn't want to know.

"If the bartender isn't your boyfriend, why don't you say yes to me? Give me a chance and get to know me. It seems you've already decided you don't like me before we've had a real conversation."

From his perspective, he was kind of right. The only times I've seen him as Jenna, he's tried talking to me, but I've been rude to him by giving him short answers or ignoring him completely. He doesn't know that I've seen him blow up after tournaments. Even so, I still had the right to tell him no without explaining myself. I sighed.

"I'm sorry, Carter. I just came here to watch Sam and—"

"Let me take you to that quiet bar down the street and we can talk," he interrupted. He stepped in closer, trying to push a strand of hair behind my ear. I flinched at his touch. I gritted my teeth, ready to tell him to back off, but then a hand landed on Carter's shoulder and pulled him backward.

"Hey man, you want to give her some space?"

"What the…" Carter stumbled then turned to see who grabbed him. "What's your problem?" He glared at Eric, who now stood between us. Taller than Carter, he blocked me from view.

"No problem. Now." Eric faced me. "You okay, Jenna?"

I took a quick breath in, trying not to gasp out loud, and drank him in wearing a forest-green Henley snug across his chest and a red beanie over his long hair. I tore my eyes from his muscles and found him frowning at me.

"Jenna?"

I blinked. "Oh, I'm fine."

"Hey, man," said Carter. "We were talking. We'll be done in a bit." He attempted to step around Eric, but Eric blocked his path.

"You're done now."

Carter stared at him for a second but then smirked. Oh no. It was the same expression Carter had before he started a tournament, his invincible look. He retreated a step, turned to me, and winked. "Next time."

I shivered. I couldn't understand why Carter wouldn't give up. I had never shown an ounce of interest. He was starting to creep me out even more than he annoyed me.

Once Carter disappeared with his friends, I turned back to Eric.

"What's his deal?" Eric asked.

"I'm not entirely sure. He won't stop asking me out, and I've all but read him the definition of no."

"Weird."

"So what brings you here?"

"Well, I have fond memories of this place. See, this amazing woman rejected me and I just love the pain."

It made me smile because at that moment it struck me that I rejected him just like Carter, except I wasn't exactly upset about seeing him again. I opened my mouth to protest, but he raised his pointer finger.

"In fact, I scared this woman so much she literally ran from the idea of ever speaking to me again."

I looked at him sheepishly. "I had a reason."

He tilted his head.

"I can't tell you. But I am sorry. And maybe we could start over?"

He studied my face. I hoped my sincerity was apparent in my expression. I had acted rashly, out of fear. There was something about Eric that piqued my curiosity, but I was too worried about him being one of Carter's buddies and knowing about the MyVid video. Although the way he'd just dealt with Carter made it clear they weren't friends.

"I suppose we could start over. I was hoping to run into you tonight."

"You were?"

"Yes." Eric had a serious look on his face, but his eyes were brighter. He turned to Sam, who was starting her next match. "What were you up to tonight?"

"Oh I..." I bit my lip for just a moment. "Sam posted that she would be playing here tonight. I wanted to see her gameplay live. Not just in her clips."

I internally kicked myself. Why was I telling him all this? I waited for him to question me more but instead he nodded.

"When you're done, do you want to get some ice cream?" Eric asked.

I glanced out the window. "Ice cream? It's freezing out. And snowing!" I sounded hysterical. How in the world could this man be craving ice cream?

Eric glanced out the window too, then shrugged.

Sam was now packing up her things.

"Come on. It's only a few blocks away."

"We're walking?"

Eric ignored my protests and led me to the door. I wrapped my scarf around my neck and pulled on my hat and gloves. I mouthed "help me" to Lewis as we passed the bar, but he just smiled and gave me a thumbs-up.

Eric swung the door open, and immediately the winter chill bit at my face. He seemed unaffected in his light jacket and paper-thin gloves. At least he had on his beanie.

He held out his arm, and I didn't hesitate to thread mine though and walked closely beside him.

"Wow, you're hot," I blurted out.

He flashed me a rare smile.

"I mean, you're really warm. Like your body is radiating heat." I blushed, realizing how I sounded, and he laughed.

"Yeah, I've always been a bit warm-blooded. It's been useful through the years."

"Useful how?"

"I spent a lot of time outside in my last job."

"Sounds like torture."

"It was fun," he said, his voice flat.

"What kind of work did you do?"

Eric stopped in front of a café. "I was a snowboarder." He winced then pushed the door open, and I rushed inside. He chuckled at me as I quickly pulled the door closed behind us.

"Oh, I've been wanting to try this place," I said.

He had brought me into Cocoa Craze. Yes, they had ice cream, but they also offered cakes, pastries, hot chocolate, and coffee. All selections included some amount of chocolate.

"What would you like?" he asked as we approached the counter.

"Hot chocolate, please."

Eric ordered one for me and a chocolate ice cream cone for himself. While they made our orders, I scanned the shop. The case that held the treats was brightly lit, while the rest of the café was cozier. There were dark oak tables and chairs for people to sit at and a tall bookshelf on the back wall with books and games for customers to borrow. The big window in the bustling street of the city's center.

The barista handed me my drink and Eric, his ice cream cone. We made our way to a table near the bookshelf in the back. I set down my drink and held his cone while he removed his coat. I passed his cone back and did the same.

We sat down and Eric took a lick of his chocolate ice cream while I took my first sip of hot chocolate.

"Oh, my goodness. This is the best hot chocolate I've ever tasted."

"I know, right?" Eric said in between licks. He was making quick work of it.

I tore my eyes from his mouth. "So snowboarding, eh?" I didn't know of many snowboarders from the Midwest, with our flatlands and four seasons.

Eric shoved the last bite of cone in his mouth and ran his hand through his hair while he chewed. Once he swallowed, he answered quietly, "Yeah. I was really into it."

"What happened?"

He blew out a breath. "I tried to pull off a huge trick in competition and crashed hard. It ruined my knee and messed up my shoulder."

I gasped. "That's horrible." Without a thought, I reached out and grabbed his hand. He squeezed it back.

"Yeah. I'm alive," he gritted out. "I'm sorry, I didn't mean to share such a depressing thing."

"No, it's fine. But it must be hard to think about. Where did you snowboard?"

"Out west. My family moved here after the accident, about

two and a half years ago. I didn't really have a reason to stay." Eric gazed out the window.

I let go of his hand and took another sip of my drink. "What do you do now?"

He looked back over at me and straightened in his chair. "I... do some freelance video editing."

"Wow, what kind of editing?"

His eyes shifted outside again. "A bit of this and that," he said to the snow. "I think I'd like to go back to school to study physical therapy. Despite everything, that was the bright light of my recovery. I'd like to help other people reach their potential. But school just isn't in the cards right now."

"Physical therapy would be a great career choice. Really rewarding."

He turned and leaned forward in his seat, meeting my eyes. They pierced me in a way that made me feel seen. "So, Jenna, you love gaming."

A statement, not a question. How did he know? I froze. If he had seen the video, I would rather know now than later.

I answered carefully. "Yes. I enjoy gaming here and there. What makes you say that?"

"I could tell by our *Space Invaders* match." He sat back and watched me as I shifted in my seat.

"I'm a little competitive." I cringed inside, regretting what I said. It was one thing that Thomas never understood. If he's like that, then...

"Cool."

"Cool?"

"Yeah. Cool. You were fun to play against."

Huh.

"Tell me a fun fact," I blurted out.

"A fun fact?"

"Yes, tell me something about yourself. It can be something fun, serious, a random childhood memory. Anything."

"Hmm. I once snowboarded down a mountain in a Speedo. Due to losing a bet. It was colder out than today."

I choked a little on my hot chocolate. "Colder? Who did you bet with?"

Eric hesitated. "My best friend. Anyway, my mom was so mad, I was grounded for two weeks except it didn't feel like it because I still had to train and I still got to see my friends."

I couldn't get the image out of my head of Eric snowboarding down a hill in what is essentially a bikini bottom with that fit body of his. I shook my head.

"What about you? What's your fun fact?"

"I've only dated two guys. One in high school and one in college." I blushed, realizing how it sounded—either an embarrassing admission or an announcement that I was indeed now available.

Eric brightened. "Why didn't they work out?"

"Why is that important?"

"I need to know what not to do."

My face was burning red. I grabbed a napkin and started twisting it. "Oh, well, the first was just a high school crush. We went out for a few months. No hard feelings. The second was in college, and, well, he didn't turn out to be who I thought he was."

I looked up at Eric. I watched his jaw tick and then it was gone.

"What about you? Any one-who-got-away stories?"

"No. Well, I mean, yes. I've dated some, but my longest relationship was my last one. She... cared more about her image than me."

"Oh, I'm sorry."

Eric smiled. "Don't be." His phone started buzzing. He glanced at it, silencing the alarm. "I'm sorry, I have to get back. Can I walk you to your car?"

"Everything okay?"

"Yes, I just have to str—work on a video edit for a client. It's due tomorrow."

"Sure." I grabbed my cup and the twisted napkin and threw them away, then bundled up again.

He stuck his hands in his pockets but didn't bother to zip his jacket. When we walked outside, he looked up at the snow falling and took a deep breath. "It's nice, isn't it?"

"I changed my mind."

He looked over at me.

"I don't know if I want to start over with an unhinged person."

He smiled and pulled out his phone. "Too late. What's your number?"

I told him my number, and we started walking.

"I'm taking my sister to breakfast Sunday. Would you like to join us?"

I ran through my plans for the weekend. Other than my shift at the coffee shop, I had Sunday free.

"Your sister?"

"Yeah, she's seventeen. It's a monthly tradition since we moved here."

He had a seventeen-year-old sister. My heart ached; that was how old my brother Matt was…

"And you're sure it's okay if I go?"

"Yeah. You two will get along great. She's super friendly. Afterward maybe you and I can do something on our own. No pressure. I'll text you the details and you can decide."

I nodded, still unsure of what to do.

We finally reached my car. I unlocked it and opened the door. Before I could get in, Eric slid his hand into mine.

"Thank you, Jenna."

"For what?"

He squeezed my hand and then let go. "For starting over."

I nodded as he walked away backward, hands in his pockets.

"Good night, Jenna," he said, as I climbed in. Then he turned and continued down the street.

Once I got home, I put on my PJs and curled up on the couch, opening Simmerz on my iPad. On Simmerz, several of my favorite female streamers were on, but so was EHucker. Instead of clicking on one of my usuals, I popped onto his stream to find him talking to his chat as he pulled up a game to play. Viewers sent in donations, which he read off and responded to.

"Jerry, you want to know the last horror game I played? Let me tell you, I screamed like a toddler running from a nest of angry hornets. Actually, I screamed like an adult running from a nest of hornets. *Loudest Dark* was no joke. You should play."

I laughed. I could relate.

"Chat, next month is March Madness. We're making brackets, but not of teams. We're making brackets of the games I'll be playing, and we'll see which one comes out on top based on how many of you show up and enjoy the game. Then I'll give away the top game to ten of you, but that's only if we meet our sub goals."

A flurry of sub donations hit the screen. I watched as the count on the face cam goal in the top corner slowly increased as well. He still had a ways to go.

He was fun to watch, even if we couldn't see him. I liked listening to his stories, and his community seemed to be positive. Of course, there are always a few trolls in the bunch, but his mods must be keeping them at bay.

I hit the donation button and sent him twenty-five dollars then saw it pop up on screen.

"Oh hey! Jenson. Twenty-five. He says, *'Be sure to include*

Loudest Dark *on your March Madness list. I'm sure newer viewers would love to see it.'* Very funny, Jenson. Maybe if you play it with me. Hit me up sometime. Okay, chat, let's get this game going." He started a *Total Command* match.

Did he just ask me to game with him? Regardless, I wasn't playing *Loudest Dark.* He was probably just joking. Besides, I didn't play with a mic anymore. Would he expect me to play on stream? No. I was getting ahead of myself. But if he was serious... it was a big deal—in the world of video game streamers, he was well known among the gaming community.

I watched his stream for a bit longer before starting up a game myself. I still wanted to practice what I had seen tonight in Sam's game. In a solo match, it would have a different feel. I didn't mind though. It was that or joining a game with random players, and I didn't want to risk running into more guys who thought this was just a guy's thing.

I was in the middle of my eighth game when a friend request popped up from EHucker360. I dropped my controller. I scrambled to pick it up when I realized I was getting shot at in my match. Too late: My character was hit, and I was eliminated from the game.

I stared at the friend request for a minute before hitting *Accept.* Seconds later, I received a message.

EHucker360: Play?

I bit my lip. Despite my excitement, I hesitated.

Jenson: Are you still streaming?

EHucker360: I'm offline.

Before I could change my mind, I told him yes, I would join his game.

EHucker360: Mic?

My heart pounded in my chest, and my breathing hollowed. I held my finger over the unmute button for a few seconds. I clenched my hand then pulled away and began typing.

Jenson: No.

EHucker360: No worries.

I blew out a sigh. I knew I'd made it harder on myself by not communicating with the team. Some people got peeved about it, depending on the game.

He loaded the match, and we played well together despite not being able to speak. He let me lead our squad, and he fought by my side effortlessly. We used pings on the map to point out enemies, directions, and supplies. To an outside viewer, it would have seemed like we were in constant communication or had been playing together for years. We had a ton of fun. After winning two games then placing third, he messaged me again.

EHucker360: I've gotta run. Thank you for indulging me, Jenson. Catch you next time.

He logged off before I could respond. But I didn't care; I was in shock.

I stared at my screen. Did that just happen? I flipped to my recent players and yup, there was his gamertag. I dropped my controller again, then yelled out excitedly to my empty house.

When I finally calmed down, I turned off my Xbox and got ready for bed. I don't know why he picked me out of the crowd, but it was the most fun I had had playing online with another person in a long time.

Chapter Six

ERIC

"Emily, are you ready?" I called out, waiting in the foyer of my parents' house. I didn't plan to stay long, and frankly, I didn't want to be there.

Growing impatient, I wandered into the living room and cringed, remembering one reason I hated coming over. Pictures of me and my sister lined the mantle, many of me standing in a winter wonderland with my snowboard and gear. Moving past the last one, my chest constricted. I snatched it off the shelf. I used to have this picture in my room. Now it was here, taunting me.

Justin and I had our arms around each other's shoulders while holding up our snowboards on each side. We used to snowboard together until my accident ruined my career. As friends we were super close; as competitors we were fierce opponents. But we made each other better.

I wondered who made him better now.

Despite the passing of time, Justin still called me twice a month, and I always let it go to voicemail.

"There you are," said Mom.

I returned the photo to its spot as she charged in and pulled me into a hug.

"Oh, I love that photo of you and Justin," she said, releasing me. "I miss him so much."

I winced at her statement. In addition to me, my dad was Justin's snowboarding coach. Justin was always at our house and to Mom, he was like another son.

"Have you talked to him lately?"

"Yes," I lied.

"Send him our love next time you talk, okay?"

"Sure."

"Sweetie, how have you been? Come and say hi to Dad." She placed a gentle hand on my back, directing me toward the kitchen.

"Mom, I really can't stay."

"Oh yes you can. Emily can wait."

I refused to tell her it wasn't my sister I was concerned about. I had texted Jenna the link to the restaurant and a time. But I hadn't heard back, so I couldn't be late in case she showed up.

Dad sat at the kitchen table, reading the newspaper and eating an omelet. The table hugged the sidewall where there was barely enough room for Mom to maneuver around the stove and counters.

"Hey, Eric," Dad said, briefly glancing up from his paper. He took another bite and refocused on his article.

Our old house in Colorado, which my sponsor money helped buy for them years ago, had a huge kitchen with an island and state-of-the-art appliances. Mom loved to host gatherings and cook on the six-burner gas stove. Now someone else enjoyed that kitchen.

"What's new?" Mom turned back to the sink to finish hand-washing the dishes.

"Not much. Been working a lot." I paused briefly, figuring out what I could offer up. "I went back to the bar."

"I'm glad you've been getting out of the apartment. Have you had any luck applying for jobs? Cindy at work said her son got a job at the bank down on 1st Street. You could check if there are any openings there." She had her back turned, but her hands rested on the sudsy bowl, waiting for my reply.

I sighed. "Mom, I have a job. Streaming is my work. Besides, you probably need a college degree to work at a bank."

"Maybe not as a teller. Or what about at the grocery store? It doesn't have to be forever. It would get you on your feet."

"Mom, I make more money streaming."

She rinsed off the bowl, set it on the drying rack, and turned to face me. "I know that. But I think it would be best if you get a job out in the world. Interact with real people. Streaming is not good for you."

I blew out a breath and pinched the bridge of my nose. "I have a big enough following that it pays for everything. Besides, snowboarding wasn't a typical job. It was a hobby that I mastered enough to make money. You never objected to that career."

Hurt flashed across her face, and I immediately regretted my words. But I was tired of arguing with her about streaming. I never went to college, but I got by on the money I made, and then some. I was slowly paying my parents back for my medical bills and trying to edge them closer to the nicer lifestyle my snowboarding career had provided. I had food and a place to live. Everything else didn't matter anymore.

"Enough," my father barked. "Eric, you will not talk to your mother that way." More gently he said, "Melissa, he knows what we think about his streaming. He will figure it out. Let him be for today."

My dad wasn't much of a talker, so when he spoke, I listened. Despite our current rift, I respected and loved my family. Dad was there when I strapped my first snowboard to my feet. I owed this to them.

"I'm sorry, Mom."

"Me too, sweetheart." With a pained expression, she turned back to the dishes.

I stayed silent, as the damage was already done.

Thankfully, Emily danced into the kitchen.

"Ready," Emily sang. She hugged me and I wrapped my arms around her, kissing the top of her head.

"What's with all frowning faces?" she asked, looking from me to Mom and Dad.

"It's nothing," I said.

She poked me in the side. "Now, now. It's a beautiful morning. Don't be a grumpy McGrumpy Pants!"

That was the pro and con of my sister. She always seemed to be in a good mood. Sometimes I loved it, and sometimes I despised it.

"Come on. Let's go." I pulled her toward the door.

Once we got in the car, I felt my chest loosen. "So... we might not be having lunch alone today."

"Oh! Did you finally make a friend? Is he cute? Do I look okay?" Emily pulled out a tube of lipstick out of her purse, pulled down the visor mirror, and started applying.

"Hey, I have friends."

She made me sound like a loser. Of course I had friends. There was the guy at the coffee house I liked chatting with about sports named... Tom? Travis? Then there was Trekster, though we hadn't met in person. And Lewis was a new friend. I should probably text him to hang out.

And then there was Justin. Whose calls I ignored. My stomach sank. My sister was right.

"First of all, you look fine, regardless of who we're meeting. Second, no. Don't even think about it. My friends are too old for you. Need I remind you that you're a teenager? Third, *she* is a woman I met, and I really like her, so don't embarrass me." I kicked over the engine.

"Oh, no."

I pulled out of the driveway and headed to the café.

"Why would you do this to me? You know I can't stand the women you date. They act nice to my face and mean behind my back. They only care about their looks and your attention."

"We're not dating, and anyway, Jenna is different. She's not like that. Not at all."

In Colorado, once I turned pro, women seemed to come out of the woodwork. It did wonders for my ego. Eventually I started dating Kara, who Emily never really clicked with. Even after several months everything felt surface level. She was only with me for my money and social status. After that was gone, so was she. I was bitter that she left me at my lowest, though I was also relieved.

Emily stared at me. "Oh, you're serious."

"Yes. I don't even know if she's coming. She didn't respond." I gripped the steering wheel tighter. Nerves jolted through me.

"She didn't respond to you? Mr. Life of the Party?" Emily teased.

I sighed heavily.

We arrived at the café right on time. I parked the car and stopped Emily before she got out. "Could you not mention my stream to her? Actually, stay away from the topic of gaming entirely."

Emily smiled. "What? You don't want her to think you're boring?"

"Gaming is not boring. Emily, please. I mean it."

Her eyes widened, and she held up her hands in surrender. "Okay, you got it, big bro. I promise I'll behave and not mention your stream. That doesn't mean I won't share other stories." Grinning mischievously, Emily got out of the car and practically skipped toward the café.

I groaned and raked my hand through my hair before pulling on my beanie. What had I gotten myself into?

I followed my sister inside and scanned the restaurant. It was a cute little place off the beaten path called Minnie's. I'd randomly discovered it one morning after a long night of streaming. The food was delicious, and the service quick.

When I spotted Jenna, my breath caught in my throat. She was sitting by the window, looking down at her phone. Seeing how her eyebrows were furrowed in concentration and how her fingers moved across the screen, I figured she was playing a game. Her hair hung over part of her face, and she wore a creamy-beige sweater with a V-neckline that accentuated her cleavage.

My sister elbowed my side. "I think I know which one is her. Come on," she said, marching toward Jenna.

I followed, feeling like the room was suddenly ten degrees warmer. Jenna looked up and set her phone down as Emily slid into the booth.

"Hi. I'm Emily. You must be Jenna. Eric told me you'd be joining us today."

I sat down, and Jenna glanced at me before responding to Emily. "Oh, um, yeah. Eric invited me the other night to join you. I hope you don't mind. I know this is your time together."

Jenna eyed me again, and I nodded to reassure her. "Hi, Jenna." I let out the breath I was holding.

"Hey, Eric," she responded with a shy smile.

I couldn't take my eyes off her.

"Of course it's okay if you join us," Emily said, breaking me from my Jenna haze.

"Sorry I didn't text, Eric. A coworker was looking for someone to cover her shift, but she ended up finding someone else."

"No problem. I'm glad you're here."

Emily propped her elbow on the table and rested her chin on her hand. "So how did you meet my brother?"

"Oh, we met at Button Mashers, the video-game bar downtown," Jenna said.

"You? Eric? At Button Mashers? That's interesting..." A slow smile slid across on her face. She opened her mouth to speak, but I nudged her leg. Hard.

"Why is that interesting?" Jenna asked Emily.

I glared at my sister. This was a disaster in the making. We had only been sitting here for two minutes and she was already going to run her mouth about the one thing I told her not to mention.

"Oh, I guess I didn't know he was into old-school games is all." I relaxed in my seat.

Jenna's eyes lit up, and she straightened her back. "I love old arcade games. My favorite is *Ms. Pacman.* I currently hold the highest score at Button Mashers. It was so cool what creators were able to develop in the gaming industry in the late seventies. And just look at where we are today, with MMOs, RPGs, FPS games, and more."

Emily's mouth had popped open. I was shocked too. Then again, when Jenna was passionate about something, her confidence and boldness emerged. I had seen it when we met, and I had seen it the other night.

"MMOs, RP what?" Emily asked.

"Massive multiplayer online, role-playing games, and first-person shooters. Sorry, I forget not everyone knows what those mean." Jenna picked up her menu and hid behind it. It seemed like whenever the topic of gaming came up, she would minimize her enjoyment of it.

"No, I think it's great you love all that." Emily glanced at me and then returned her attention to Jenna, coaxing her back into conversation.

They were hitting it off, talking about games, my sister's dancing, and the best places to shop, only pausing to order our food and then eat it. I sat quietly and shoveled my ham-and-veggie omelet into my mouth, taking pleasure in their camaraderie.

Emily twisted toward me. "Eric, I haven't caught up with you yet. How are you? I'm glad to see you've gotten out of your apartment."

"Jeez, Em, you make it sound like I'm a hermit." I glanced at Jenna, who quietly poured more syrup on her pancakes.

Emily rolled her eyes. "Well, I did want to tell you... Justin texted me."

"Why?" I snapped.

Emily shrunk back in her seat. "He's worried about you. Why don't you talk to him?"

"No."

"But—"

"I said no!" Then I lowered my voice: "Why is he calling you, Em?"

"We talk sometimes. I miss him. I'm not ending our relationship just because of you."

I choked for a second on my bite of omelet. "Excuse me? Relationship?"

"Don't be an idiot. You know what I mean."

I felt guilty. Justin was like a brother to her too. I couldn't blame her for missing him. I preferred if she didn't talk to him, but obviously I couldn't stop her.

I rubbed my temples. "Please tell me you don't talk about me."

"Well, a little. But just the basics. He knows you're alive and well. Mainly we discuss school, dance, and snowboarding."

A sharp pain stabbed me in the chest. I removed my hat and ran my hand through my hair. Jenna's eyes flicked to my forehead, where my scar was, and I quickly pulled my hat back on. She looked down at her pancakes then took another bite.

"He misses you, and I know you miss him. Get over yourself and call him back."

"I can't. Excuse me for a minute."

I made a beeline for the restroom, splashed some water on my face, and took some deep breaths. First the picture, and now finding out Emily and Justin were talking all the time? I leaned on the sink, staring at myself in the mirror. "You're fine. Don't think about it. Think about Jenna."

Jenna! I left her at the table with my sister. Who knew what Emily was telling her. I dried my hands and made my way back to the table. Jenna was laughing. My worst fears confirmed—Emily must have told her everything. Yet she was still here. That had to count for something.

"Once he realized his pants had split, he just stood there, holding me in the air while everyone had a view of his backside."

I plopped back down in my seat, relieved. Her dance partner's pants had split during a performance.

"Wait, was he not wearing underwear?" Jenna asked.

"Nope. Or he was wearing a man thong. So the lines wouldn't show during a performance."

Jenna giggled again.

"Welcome back, big bro."

I nodded, and Jenna shared a small smile with me.

After checking her phone, Emily nudged me. "I've gotta go," she said, sliding out of our booth. "Sarah's here to pick me up. It was great to meet you, Jenna. Sorry, I have to leave you with this grump." She smiled and I frowned.

Emily leaned down to hug Jenna goodbye and bounced out the door.

We sat there quietly as Jenna sipped her coffee. I couldn't help but stare into her brown eyes.

She set her mug down. "So, not to upset you, but can I ask who Justin is?"

Maybe Emily didn't rat me out. "I'm sorry about that. I didn't mean to lose my temper. He's my best friend. Or was. I'm not sure anymore."

"Was? What did he do?"

I took a long swig of water. "Justin and I grew up together in Colorado. We both strapped on our first snowboards the same week. In the beginning, we were just learning the sport, having fun together. As we got older, our talents became evident, and we both went pro. We in one moment cheered each other on and in the next, hoped that our tricks were better than the other. If it weren't for each other, we wouldn't have made it that far."

The pressure in my chest returned. I squeezed my fist tight on the table. Jenna reached out and set her palm over my closed hand and gently rubbed her thumb over it. Turning my palm up, I released the tension. She set her hand on top of mine and we cupped our hands together. I relaxed.

"But then the accident happened, and you moved away?"

"Yeah, it's..." I swallowed thickly. I couldn't put into words how I felt about Justin. I loved him and yet it was too painful to speak with him. So days turned to weeks, into months, into years. Yet he still called. "It's a long story."

"It sucks when you lose the thing you love most." There was a sadness in Jenna's eyes I hadn't seen before. I wondered what she had lost, but I had already brought the mood of the day down. Twice.

"Do you like bowling?"

Her eyes brightened, and she smiled at me. "Love it."

"Great. Let's go."

Chapter Seven

JENNA

Since we drove separately, we met at the bowling alley. Once inside, the sound of crashing pins rang out all around us.

"I haven't been bowling in years," I said.

Eric scanned the lanes. A couple of people on one, some families, and a group in matching shirts that looked to be a part of a bowling league. Our bowling alley has been around in this town since 1981. They had made some updates with electronic scoring and better lighting, but it still had the same old tables and black carpet with neon shapes.

"This is great. I haven't played in years either."

"Really? What made you want to come here?" A little boy pushed his ball down a mobile ramp and it glided straight down the lane.

"Actually, it's a stupid reason." The kid's family cheered for him after getting a strike. "My ex didn't think bowling was classy enough for her. We even had a modern bowling alley where we grew up, with neon lights and an arcade, kind of like Button Mashers. It was really cool, but she thought the shoes were gross and the atmosphere was cheesy. For some reason, this just popped into my head."

"Ah, that ex. Well, I think I look pretty great in bowling shoes. Let's go have fun." I smiled at Eric. He reciprocated with an amused look and followed me to the shoe counter.

Once we paid for our games and shoe rentals, we picked out our bowling balls, and took them to our lane. We removed our coats and draped them over the chairs. After getting his bowling shoes on, Eric sat at the scoring computer.

"Do you want to go first?" he asked, entering my name in the computer.

"Doesn't matter. Just prepare to lose," I said while tying my laces.

"I don't know about that."

I gave him a sly grin, then stepped up to the lane and hoisted my ball. I swung my arm back then forward, and let it go. I knocked down a couple of pins. On my second throw, I struck down two more.

"Watch and learn," Eric teased as he stepped up.

I plopped down on the chair and crossed my arms.

Eric glanced back at me then started to bowl. I watched his muscles flex as he swung his arm back. The thunk of his ball going straight into the gutter snapped me out of my trance. I burst out laughing.

He waited for his ball to return up the chute then grabbed it. He tried again and hit only one pin.

"What was I supposed to learn?" I asked innocently.

"You learned what you shouldn't do."

"Sure, sure. My turn," I said, getting up.

As it turned out, neither of us was great at bowling. We competed the best we could in the first game, but our scores were both low. Eric somehow won by eight points.

I pouted in my seat, but he lifted my chin and met my eyes.

"Don't be sad. I have a better idea for the next game."

"What?" I asked, narrowing my eyes.

His eyes darted to my lips, and he swallowed before moving back to the monitor. He pressed Start for the next game, which cleared our scores. He then snatched up his ball and faced me.

"The name of the game is called Match Me. We take turns bowling in weird ways, and the other person has to replicate it."

He walked backward, and flung the ball behind him down the lane.

My mouth flew open as he hit eight pins.

He shrugged. "My friends and I played like this more often than regular bowling."

"I love it."

We bowled the next game with goofy poses and dance moves, constantly cracking up. In the end, the score didn't matter.

We returned our shoes and bowling balls then got sodas at the concession stand and sat down at a table overlooking the lanes.

"Y'know, I haven't enjoyed playing a game with a guy in a long time, so thank you."

"Was our game at Button Mashers not fun?"

This was it. I could take the leap and trust him or make excuses and move on. Yet hiding was exhausting. Maybe for once I wanted to be seen, but that didn't mean it would be easy.

"It was. That was also not something I often do. I mostly mean I don't normally play video games online with guys anymore. At least not with mics."

"Why not?"

"It's a long story. Have you ever heard of Trained Girl?

"No…"

"Good. I mean, well, don't look it up. Basically, my college boyfriend made a really awful compilation video of my gaming and clipped together moments where he told viewers with voiceover commentary, how to fix my terrible gameplay. It went viral. You haven't seen it?"

"Wow. No. Ex-snowboarder, remember? It was my whole existence."

Eric ran his hand through his hair and then stared at the empty bowling lane. He turned and met my eyes.

"I'm really sorry that happened, Jenna."

"Thank you. That's why I don't want to play with random guys online or go out with guys that are only into video games."

Eric's jaw ticked, but then he took a sip of his soda, and I thought I'd imagined it.

Suddenly a weight had been lifted off me. I never told anyone about the video. Normally I didn't have to; you could say "Trained Girl," and everyone knew what that was.

Eric leaned forward and took my hand.

"You know not all guys who play games online are like that, right?"

"Honestly, I don't know. But even if there are good guys, I'm not sure if it's worth the risk. I have to act a certain way to be respected. I have to play well, and if I get mad, I get called out while a guy getting mad at the game is funny."

That video really messed with my head. I used to watch my brother game all the time, and now I wondered how he talked to other people online. I shook my head. No, I refused to see him in a different way because of what that idiot Thomas did.

"Actually, I lied," I said. "I did play a game with someone online the other night and had fun. He was a streamer, but he uses a voice changer. I requested to not use mics, but we played really well together. It was awesome."

I couldn't contain my excitement. Eric appeared to study me for a moment.

"Sorry," I said, turning pink. "After what my ex did, it was a bit of a milestone for me."

Eric looked as lost in thought as I was. Suddenly he stood up, grabbed his empty cup, and tossed it in the trash. "Sounds like this guy might be okay. Try talking to him if you game again. Maybe it'll give you courage to put yourself out there."

"Okay."

"Are you ready to go? I have some work I need to finish."

I stood up as well and threw my empty cup away. "Thanks again for today. I'll see you later?"

"Definitely."

"Order for Ella!" I called, setting two full drink holders down.

A young woman scurried to the counter, stacked the cardboard holders, and picked everything up.

"Got it?" I asked.

"Yes. No worries. I've totally got this."

Her heels clicked against the floor as she rushed out the door with a mountain of drinks. I hoped it was a short walk for her.

It took everything to drag myself out of bed this morning to get to Three Beans Coffee Shop downtown. Last night I had fallen asleep on the couch, controller in hand, before moving to my bed at 2 a.m. The shop was cutely named after the owners' triplet babies, whom they called their three little beans. It was also an excellent pun that brought joy to my nerdy heart.

The morning work crowd had finally thinned out, allowing me a chance to breathe. I wiped down the counter and restocked the supplies. I added cups to the stacks and checked that all the syrups were full.

"Did you kick butt last Wednesday?" my coworker Rita asked me.

Just a couple of years older than me, Rita clicked with me right away. She recently married her boyfriend of five years, who was some sort of *Dungeons and Dragons* extraordinaire, and apparently she enjoyed it too, among other board games. Though our mediums were different, we bonded over our love of games. But she was a lot spunkier than I was, and more outspoken. You could not put her and Alyssa in a room together if you ever wanted to talk.

"Yes," I said quietly while stocking the fridge with milk and cream.

"Don't be shy. You should be excited. You're a great gamer. At least I assume with how often you come in here telling me about your latest wins."

"Thanks, Rita." As we had gotten to know each other, it inevitably came out that I participated in video game tournaments. But she didn't know I played them as Jenson or that I was too afraid to put myself out there.

"Heads up. Looks like it's time for your break." Rita nodded toward the door as it chimed, and Bryan entered, pulling off his gloves. He came in twice a week during my break, and we used that time to catch up.

I grabbed a cup to make his usual chai latte. He handed Rita a ten-dollar bill. Rita made his change, which he shoved into the tip jar.

Rita offered him a toothy grin. "I knew I liked you, Jenna's male BFF."

Bryan laughed easily at her comment. I passed him his drink, poured some water for myself, and joined him at our usual spot by the window.

Once we graduated from college, it was hard to shift from seeing each other every day as friends and coding partners to hardly at all. Even though Alyssa and he were dating, it was still important to maintain my friendship with Bryan. Thankfully, his work schedule was flexible, so he was usually able to meet up with me.

He sipped his coffee then asked, "How is it going?"

I shrugged. "Fine."

"Okay, what's wrong?"

"What do you mean?"

"Jenna, *fine* is the universal code women use to tell men when they're exactly the opposite of fine."

I sighed heavily. "Okay, fine." Bryan opened his mouth, but I held up my hands. "I saw Eric again. Twice."

"How? I thought you said you didn't give him your number."

"I didn't. He showed up at Button Mashers."

"Uh-huh."

"I was checking out this great gamer, who had posted she'd be there Friday night. I was watching, really into the match, when Carter came over and hit on me."

"Again?" Bryan wrinkled his nose.

"Yeah, and he was being extra creepy. Anyway, Carter touched my hair and, before I could register what was happening, Eric had pulled him back. Then Eric invited me out for ice cream—well, I had hot chocolate—and we got to talking. I decided we could just start over, so now we have each other's number."

Bryan smiled ever so slowly. "You like him. When was the second time?"

"Sunday morning. I had breakfast with him and his younger sister, and then he and I went bowling."

"Wow. That is a turn of events since the last time we talked."

"I also told Eric about the *trained girl* video."

Bryan's eyes went as wide as saucers. "That's... What did he say?"

"Not a lot. He seemed upset about it. He said he was sorry that happened to me and encouraged me to give gaming with guys online another shot."

"I agree," Bryan said, and sipped his coffee.

"Well, I sort of have. I played a duo match the other night."

That woke Bryan up. He set his coffee down. "My goodness, Jenna. With who?"

"I don't know."

"You played with a random? That's still great. I'm proud of you."

I fiddled with my work apron. "Actually, he's a streamer. After I sent a message into his stream, he asked me to hit him up for a game."

"That's... interesting. Which streamer? Wait, did you play *while* he was streaming? Do I know him?" He grabbed his phone and started scrolling.

"No, he wasn't streaming. He's sort of a mystery."

Bryan's thumb paused, hovering above his screen. "Wait. Do you mean EHucker?"

I sat back in my chair and gazed out the window, trying to avoid Bryan's scrutiny.

"Wow, Jenna. Are you serious?"

"Dead. We played amazingly together. You know he uses a voice changer, and I don't use my mic, so we messaged before and after. I don't know why he asked me out of everyone in his chat, but we won our game."

I took a long drink of water to distract myself from the fact that I was way too excited about EHucker. I knew nothing about the guy, and yet I was gushing over our one little victory. I couldn't help it. I was passionate about gaming and thrilled I was able to complete a duo match without totally freaking out about being paired with a random guy.

"What?" I asked, noticing the tight expression on his face.

"Nothing." He hesitated. "It's odd he randomly messaged you to play. I don't watch a ton of streamers, but from what I know about him, he rarely plays with anyone outside of Trekster and a few others."

"I know."

"And this was your first time in his stream?"

"Yes, but—"

"Huh."

"What do you mean, 'huh'?"

"Just be careful, Jenna. No one truly knows who EHucker is."

I knew this and wondered the same things everyone else did. As popular as he was, the number of subscribers he needed to use his face cam was still very high. I knew why I kept to myself, but what was his deal?

"I'll be okay," I reassured Bryan.

"And let me know if Eric pulls anything. I'll kick his butt."

"Come on, Bryan, you know that's not true."

"You're right. I would sic Alyssa on him so I wouldn't have to."

I chuckled, knowing it was true. Eric wouldn't stand a chance if Alyssa came after him.

"Speaking of," Bryan said, "did you tell Alyssa about it?"

"Not yet."

"Please do. You know I hate keeping secrets from her."

"True. I will after my shift. I'm meeting up with her to watch a movie. So enough about me, what is going on with you?"

Bryan's whole demeanor changed. He sat back in his seat and crossed his arms.

"Nothing," he said, scowling at the table.

"Bryan."

"Okay, fine. I know Alyssa is waiting for me to propose. I'm ready to do it, but every time I think of how, it's not good enough, or I can't seem to catch her off guard. She drops hints constantly."

"Aw, Bryan!" I clapped my hands together. "Do you have a ring?"

"Yes, and I carry it around all the time in case a perfect moment presents itself. Every time I start to gain confidence, she gives me that look—the one that tells me she would love for this to be the moment—and I end up getting cold feet."

"Can I see it?"

Bryan checked over his shoulder like he was worried Alyssa could be watching. He discreetly handed me the ring box. I flipped open the small black velvet top, and there sat a beautiful yellow-gold ring with three round diamonds glistening from the light streaming in through the window.

"Wow," I said, breathless. "She's going to love it." I handed him back the ring, and he pocketed it.

"What do I do, Jenna?" Bryan dropped his head in his hands looking defeated.

I snapped my fingers. "Hey." He looked up at me. "Listen, I know Alyssa wants to marry you. Obviously. She won't care how you propose as long as you propose. I say quit looking for the perfect moment and *find* a moment. And I'll get her to lay off the hint dropping."

"I don't want her to know we talked about it."

"Of course. I'll bring it up casually, and she won't think a thing about it."

"Thanks, Jenna."

I checked the time. I had gone over on my break by a couple of minutes, and though the shop was dead, I didn't want to leave Rita hanging. "I have to get back to work. Thank you for listening to me."

Bryan got up to leave, tossed his coffee cup in the trash, and smiled. "Same. Anytime."

I grabbed a wet rag and got back to cleaning the counter while Rita took her break.

My mind wandered between Eric and EHucker. Besides being attracted to Eric, there was a level of comfort with him that allowed me to open up. Somehow I could relax around him and have fun. But I wanted to know more about him—sometimes he had that faraway look. And he had encouraged me to try gaming online again. Maybe I would, because I had felt like myself playing with EHucker. I did find it odd that he would ask me to game out of the blue. Did I cross his path in another stream, somehow making me stand out from the rest?

"Yo, Jenna. I think the counter is clean," Rita called out, coming back from her break.

"Right."

Whatever I did next, one thing was true: I went from brushing off guys completely to interacting with two in one week. And one I had yet to speak to.

Chapter Eight

ERIC

After pushing the door to my office open, I stared at my setup and sighed. I plopped down in front of my computer and logged in to my bank. After seeing last month's earnings, I transferred most of it to my parents' account, only leaving enough for food and rent for me. I sat back, running my hand down my face.

Later I had a stream with Trekster. We were hosting a tournament for our communities, wanting to give back to the people who showed up every day and subscribed to our channels. We had pooled together some prize money, so participation was high. We weren't playing, but we were going to watch and comment on our viewers' gameplay. The tournament was expected to run late, and I was already exhausted—my two trips to Button Mashers were out of the norm and I had been doing overtime to make up for it. If I didn't stay engaged, it would be easy for my viewers to get hooked into another community, and ultimately I'd lose my income.

My phone vibrated on my desk. I glanced at the screen: Justin. I closed my eyes and took a few breaths. Hitting the *Ignore* button, I tossed my phone aside and stepped barefooted onto the balcony—into an inch of snow. Thick snowflakes fell onto my eyelids, bare chest, and mouth. I ran my tongue across my lips, tasting the fresh ice.

My body grew as numb as I felt inside. I tried to clear my head, but only chaos ensued. Images of mountains, Justin's face hidden behind goggles, broken bones, hours of recovery, and the tears my mother cried when we sold our house and moved away all flashed through my mind. Video game controllers, screens, scrolling chat, arcade games, and finally Jenna's face appeared.

The flashes of memories calmed as I focused on her face, and I began to feel peaceful. She was trying to prove something I didn't think she needed to. There would always be rude people on the internet, but there were some great communities as well. I hoped that I could show that to her, though I could never tell her.

My finger hovered over MyVid on my phone. I told her I wouldn't watch it, but I burned to know what that idiot said to steal some of her light.

I typed in *trained girl* and searched. The first result was the video. I pressed the triangle to play.

A college-aged kid with dark swooped hair and stud earrings appeared on screen. This must be Thomas. "MyVid! What's up? Ever play your favorite video game with your girl and this happens?" The video cut to a character falling and Jenna screaming, "No!"

"Today I'm gonna tell you how to train your girl to become a good gaming partner." The punk shrugged. "Or at least try."

My stomach turned, but I watched for a few more minutes. The rest of the video cut from her playing badly to him "providing instructions." Halfway through, I had seen enough.

I tucked my phone into my pocket and ran my hand through my hair. No wonder she went underground. If I ever saw this guy...

A harsh wind whipped me in the face, and I was knocked back to the present, realizing how cold I had become.

Cursing, I stepped back inside and shut the door. My toes burned their way back to life. I pulled a Henley over my head and put on thick socks. Returning to my office, I checked my email. I clicked on a new email from Simmerz:

EHucker360,

You are formally invited to this year's Simmerz Grand Convention. We are asking streamers across the board to participate in the competition and partner with a tournament winner from our state competitions. Your popularity in the Simmerz community is advantageous, as we donate a portion of ticket sales to charity. More details on the convention and tournament are attached. We look forward to seeing you.

I clicked into all the attached PDFs. One outlined the vendors, booths, and entertainment, while another described the tournament. The prize for placing first was $250,000. My eyes bugged out. Even divided by a team of three, it was a ton of money—not unlike the sponsorship money I used to get. My parents would be set. I could pay off my medical bills too.

I could quit streaming.

Then do what? I wasn't a snowboarder, and I was barely a gamer. Yes, I was good, but any success I've had has been pure luck. Honestly, I didn't understand why people showed up for my stream. Even with thousands of viewers a day, I was still flabbergasted by it. And winning would allow me to quit before reaching my face cam goal. No one would ever have to know.

Even so, the chance of winning was slim. That was highly dependent on who you were partnered with. I closed the email and logged on to see if Jenna/Jenson was online. She was playing my game of choice, *Total Command.*

My pulse quickened as I typed out a message. I had time for a few games before my stream. And now, I was determined more than ever to show her that not everyone was like her jerk of an ex.

EHucker360: Game?

I tapped my fingers on my desk while I waited for her to reply. Seconds later a message popped through.

Jenson: Yes.

EHucker360: Mics?

I waited a full minute for her response. I clicked on my voice changer, hoping she'd say yes. Maybe something I said to her while bowling would give me a shot.

Jenson: Why?

EHucker360: Why what?

Jenson: Why did you pick me to play with out of all your viewers?

I paused. Maybe I could play it off.

EHucker360: Need someone to play Loudest Dark *with.*

Suddenly her voice rang though my headset.

"I am *not* playing *Loudest Dark.*"

I laughed. "With me? Or just ever?"

"Ever." A moment of silence. "Nice to meet you," she said quietly.

"Same. So where do you want to land?"

"Tall guy," she declared.

Tall guy was the biggest building on the map. It was also a popular spot to land. I admired her confidence.

"You got it!"

We jumped into the game and played without speaking much except to communicate our next moves, enemy locations, and plans of attack. She led decisively and aggressively like last time and we moved as a unit, across the map. By the time we hit the fourth game, she started a different conversation with me.

"You're really good. How long have you been gaming?"

"I've casually gamed my whole life. My first love was the N64. All the Mario games, *Star Fox, Zelda.* I've only done it seriously in the last three years."

"I love N64. My brother and I played together all time growing up. It was a fun way to hang out together."

"Oh yeah? Do you game with him still?"

No response.

"Jenson?"

"Sorry. No. We don't game together anymore."

Shoot, did I say something wrong? Before I could understand what, she was talking again.

"Why don't you share your voice or face with anyone? I'm a random person somewhere in the world, and you're a random guy somewhere. I wouldn't know you."

I frowned. She would know me. This is the first time I had done this, invited someone to play with me who I knew in real life. Even Trekster hadn't heard my real voice since the first time we spoke.

"It's complicated," I replied, hoping she didn't press on, but—

"Pfft. That is the most evasive answer anyone could say."

"Fine. There would be repercussions I'd rather avoid."

At this point, our game had ended, and we were sitting on the lobby screen.

"Are... are you in trouble?" she asked.

"No, nothing like that. I'm all clear with the law." Funny she would go there. To get in trouble with the law would require going out. I took a drink of water.

"Are *you* trouble?" she asked, and I could hear her muffled giggling.

I did a spit take.

"Oh! Are you okay?"

"I sure hope so." I was *in* trouble; Jenna was a mystery to me and the more that we talked, the more I wanted to know more.

"Sorry, that was weird."

"You're fine. You just surprised me. No, I'm a very boring guy. No trouble here."

She was quiet, and I suspected she was being shy again. I glanced at the clock and realized I needed to wrap it up so I could stream with Trekster.

"I have one more question," she said.

"Shoot."

"You use a voice changer. I'm just curious how old you are. Sorry, I know you're not supposed to ask that on the internet, but if you're a teenager or maybe you're older, and well, I'm twenty-three. I just want to know—wait, you did say you played N64? But that doesn't mean anything, really, retro is in..."

Her rambling made me smile. "Jenson, it's okay. I'm twenty-five. No harm, no foul."

"I-I..." she stuttered. "Okay, cool."

I laughed again. It reminded me of the other night at Button Mashers. I didn't want to mess this up again.

"Okay," she said finally. "Thanks. For messaging me tonight."

"Of course." I checked the time once more. "Well, I have to start my stream. I'm hosting a competition with Trekster. But Jenson? Message me on Discord sometime so we can chat."

Discord was a platform many gamers used to communicate without having to chat in-game. People could also create groups to foster a sense of community.

"Okay. Have a good stream, Hucker."

"Good night, Jenson."

After getting a cup of coffee, I fired up my stream. All I had to do was press *Go Live*.

Trekster was already logged on. Moments later, he joined me in my Discord and began our voice chat.

"Hey bro, what's up?"

"Not much. Just the usual grind."

"Man, I hear ya. Ever since *Tribal* released, I've been putting in long shifts with the squad, trying it out. My girlfriend is really into this one."

"Yeah, that's streaming for ya. It ebbs and flows based on what's popular. Game any good?"

"Dude, it's tight. Lots of action. Great graphics. Easy to jump in with friends. If you ever want on our team, hit me up."

I probably would join him. Before I was a streamer, I used to watch Trekster late at night when I couldn't sleep. He made me a moderator as he started growing, and our friendship grew as well. He didn't know I was a pro snowboarder, but when my career ended, he suggested I start my own stream. Good timing.

"Anyway," Trekster continued, "we're going to take a break from it soon, take my girl out somewhere really special for her birthday. It's all about quality time."

"It's the charm, right?" I laughed. I had the opposite problem: too much time on my hands.

"Of course. What about you? Have you met anyone lately? I noticed you skipped some of your usual stream nights."

I didn't realize he would notice. However, he spent as much time streaming as I did, so if anyone was going to notice, it would be him.

He was my closest friend in the streaming community. We got along well because he was very laid back and rarely flustered by much. People enjoyed his stream because he was good at the games he played, but he also remembered things about his subscribers and genuinely cared about his viewers.

"Actually, I did meet someone."

"Really, bro? Awesome! A gamer chick or IRL?"

"Both."

"Two women?"

"No, she's the same person. She doesn't know who I am on here though." I winced, wondering if I'd revealed too much. But it was a relief to confide in someone I trusted.

"Dude. Bro. You know what, whatever man. It's great that you met someone. But if she likes you IRL, why keep hiding?"

I thought of the MyVid video. It was too late. She would never trust me if I told her now. And eventually EHucker would cease to exist anyway. My chest tightened at the thought of losing my friendship with Trekster. If I just disappeared...

"I'll figure it out" was all I could manage.

"I know you will. My Discord is always open if you need to get in touch."

"Thanks."

"All right, bro, let's start the tourney."

We both flipped on our streams and got straight to commentating.

I would have to think about Jenna/Jenson and the mess I had gotten myself into later. For now, I had a job to do.

Chapter Nine

JENNA

I found myself at Button Mashers again. Bryan and Alyssa wanted to hang out, and they suggested we come here. They knew I couldn't refuse to meet at my favorite place. I texted Eric, who said he had a couple of things to do but would try to meet us later.

Though Tuesdays were slower, Lewis still kept busy with his regulars. The bar was closed on Sunday and Monday nights for a break and bar restocks, so Tuesdays always kicked off a new week. Except for one other manager, Lewis ran the bar most of the time.

I sat on a barstool, waiting for my friends. Alyssa and I had a movie night and I updated her on everything regarding Eric and EHucker. My finger hovered over EHucker's name on Discord before I finally clicked on it and typed out a message.

Jenson: I had fun last night!

EHucker360: Me too.

I winced, thinking about our previous conversation. Did I ask him too many questions? Then I started overanalyzing our match.

Three dots appeared on screen. I held my breath.

EHucker360: It was actually a breath of fresh air to play a match with you. Normally if I'm gaming, I'm streaming. Or I'm playing with other streamers who also have their communities to talk to and multitask with. It was nice to just play with someone without all the extra noise.

Jenson: I understand. I have to admit, I was nervous when you asked me to play, but I'm glad I did.

EHucker360: Don't be nervous. Next time call me on Discord. Game chat can be finicky.

I flexed my fingers. Next time? Bryan's warning ran through my mind: "No one truly knows who EHucker is." Why me? But I didn't want to ask him again for fear of ruining whatever this was.

EHucker360: What are you up to?

Jenson: Meeting some friends at a cool arcade/gaming brewery. Are you streaming tonight?

EHucker360: Not until late.

Jenson: Okay, I'll be watching.

EHucker360: That doesn't sound creepy at all...

I laughed.

Jenson: You know what I mean!

EHucker360: I do. Have a great evening, Jenson.

I closed my messages.

Lewis walked over and set a Coke in front of me. "What's with the grin? What happened to my sad little bar flower?"

"Bar flower?" I shoved my phone in my purse and pulled the drink in close for a sip.

"Yeah, you know, like a wallflower except you sit at my bar instead."

I pursed my lips and shook my head.

"Were you texting Eric? How is that going?" Lewis asked, leaning one elbow on the bar.

"I wasn't texting Eric. Though he might stop by tonight. I was messaging..."

Lewis raised his eyebrows.

"EHucker," I said with a sigh.

"The famous streamer? How the heck did that happen?"

"I don't know. I sent him a dono one night, and the next thing I know he wants to play a match with me. We've played a couple of times, and I messaged him on Discord. It's not a big deal." Oh it was a big deal.

"I have so many questions for you. I'll start with, What about Eric?"

"He's great. This is different. EHucker is just an internet friend, an acquaintance. I don't know yet. But, for the first time in years, I feel good—safe—gaming with a stranger. He was fine with who I am."

"Uh-huh, many people are fine with you."

"And Eric, he…"

"I'm what?"

I twisted around to the man standing behind me. Eric looked extra handsome, in an olive-green nylon coat, dark-washed jeans, and boots. I was relieved to see him wearing a proper coat for once. On his head was his signature beanie—gray this time—and his hair covered the scar I'd spotted.

"You're here!" I said, getting up from my seat, and he pulled me into a hug.

I pressed my nose into his shoulder and inhaled pine and sandalwood. I half wondered when the season passed if he would still smell like this, if it was a scent that was his alone.

"I'm here," he said, letting go, and then sat down next to me. He removed his coat and draped it over the barstool, before sitting down.

"You look good."

"Thanks. You look beautiful." His lips tugged up into only a half smile but his whole face looked happy.

I sucked in a breath. The attention he gave me was disorienting and overwhelming. I didn't know if I would ever get used to it. I faced the bar and blushed. Before I knew it, an arm snaked around my waist.

"Guess who," a voice sang.

I spun around to hug Alyssa. Bryan waited behind her. I greeted them both, then introduced them to Eric.

Alyssa pulled him into an embrace. "Eric! It's so great to meet you. I've heard so much about you." Then she leaned in to whisper, not so subtly, in my ear: "Jenna, you downplayed him. He is sexy with a capital S."

Eric smiled, and Bryan said, "Lys, you're killing me."

"I mean for Jenna." She turned and wrapped her arms around Bryan. He reluctantly curled an arm around her but with a smile.

If I wasn't red before, I was surely a tomato now.

Bryan reached out a hand to shake Eric's. They ordered drinks at the bar while Alyssa told me about a prank that happened at work. Then we split off to go play in the arcade. Bryan and Eric walked toward a fighting game. Alyssa and I grabbed a spot at *Ms. Pac-Man*.

"So..." Alyssa started. "I do plan on finding out more about Eric, but have you spoken with the mystery man you told me about?"

I groaned. "Please don't torment Eric."

"You know I won't. Besides, Bryan is gathering intel. Now stop avoiding my question."

I sighed. Alyssa wouldn't drop this until I gave her details.

"I played a game with him last night, with mics on, and tonight I messaged him on Discord." I turned to start the game.

"Let me see." I unlocked my phone and handed it to Alyssa. She pulled up my message with EHucker. "That's it? Real spicy, Jen," she said sarcastically.

"Give that back." I snatched my phone. "I'm not trying to be spicy. He's a friend. A gamer friend." I glanced over at Eric, who was bent over, playing his game with Bryan.

Alyssa didn't understand. It wasn't a question of liking Eric *or* EHucker. I liked them both, but for entirely different reasons. I was crushing on Eric, but EHucker was opening up a part of my heart that I had closed off, offering me a sense of security in the wonderful world of gaming online. A place where I could be myself without judgement.

"Okay, fine. Plus, what would you want with some random internet guy when you have all of that standing over there? You should make a move on him."

I eyed Eric again. His shirt was stretched across his muscular back. I bit my lip.

"I do like Eric, but I don't make moves. I awkwardly stumble."

"Then awkwardly stumble into his arms. I'm going to go make sure he asks you on another date."

"Another date? We've just hung out—those weren't dates." My eyes widened at the idea.

Alyssa clapped her hand to my shoulder. "Oh sweetie, I know you've only dated Mr. Loser Town, but ice cream? Bowling? Those are definitely dates."

I stared at her, absorbing her words. She winked at me and took off, prancing toward Bryan and Eric.

"Alyssa, don't!" I whisper-shouted.

She waited patiently for their game to end before craning her neck to say something in Eric's ear. Great.

I checked my phone and saw I had a Discord message from EHucker360: *What kind of games are at the arcade brewery?* I replied: *All types. I like to play the classics.* Space Invaders, Ms. Pac-Man, *etc.*

I felt a tap on my shoulder. "Do you want another drink?" Eric asked.

"I'm good, thanks," I said, holding up my glass.

Eric nodded and headed toward the bar.

A minute later, I got a ping for a new message.

EHucker360: I bet I could get a higher score on Ms. Pac-Man.

A bet. Interesting. What could I have him do if I win?

Jenson: Oh, do you? What do you want to bet?

EHucker360: If I win, tell me a secret.

I looked up. Eric was leaning over the bar, talking to Lewis while he poured drinks. I looked back at my phone and typed.

Jenson: Hmm, okay, but if I win, you should stream Puppy Paws Adventure.

EHucker360: Seriously? Okay. You're on! You're still at that arcade brewery right?

I raised my eyebrows.

Jenson: Yes...

EHucker360: Then I challenge you to play a game with some-one there.

Jenson: Why?

EHucker360: No particular reason. I always find it fun playing a game against or with someone new. Good night, Jenson.

I pocketed my phone and couldn't help but think he was partly referring to us playing together for the first time. I don't know why he challenged me to play with someone at the brewery, but I knew just who I would ask. I rejoined the happy couple.

"Come on, Bryan, I want a good burger. Let's hit up Luke's Place."

"No Lys, I'm telling you, everyone is trying The Rasteraunt."

"What kind of name is that?"

Bryan shrugged. "Something to do with computers. The owner's obsessed with them. But he's also an amazing chef. The whole place has a technology-through-the-ages theme."

"I've tried it," I chimed in. "Delicious salmon. Interesting atmosphere." Patrons could choose to solve a code on an iPad to place their orders, *just for fun.*

"Fine, we'll try it," she said to Bryan.

"What's going on?" Eric asked, approaching. He handed Bryan another beer.

"Bryan and I were just deciding where to eat."

Eric grimaced. "Ah, the never-ending daily mystery."

"I know, right?" Alyssa said, nodding vigorously. "Do you guys want to come with?"

I glanced at Eric. "No, we're good. Actually, I wanted to challenge you to a game, Eric." No, he wasn't a random guy at the bar, but I'll count it.

Eric's eyes flared to life. "Of course."

"I'm hungry. We're gonna go," Alyssa said.

"But..." Bryan pointed to his fresh beer.

Alyssa grabbed it and chugged it. "There. Let's go."

Bryan made a sputtering sound and followed her.

I shook my head. "So, which game?"

Eric led me over to a car racing game, where two people sat side by side and steered with a wheel. It wasn't a classic, but Lewis got a good deal, so he'd found a spot for it near the back.

Each race was close, but Eric ended up winning.

He turned to me in the chair. "Can I take you on a date? Saturday?"

I blinked, surprised at his sudden request. "Yes," I said breathlessly.

He gazed at me, his lips inches from mine.

"Did Alyssa tell you to do this?" His eyebrows furrowed. Guess not. "Never mind. She was teasing me earlier."

"Alyssa and Bryan are great. No, she didn't tell me to ask you out." He ran a hand over his head, removing his beanie. "I wanted to." He hesitated. "Did you want me to?"

That vulnerability was back. He looked unsure yet hopeful.

"Yes, of course," I said quickly. But then I looked down. "It's just that Alyssa said our other hangouts were dates, and well, I thought we were just getting to know each other. Either way, it's fine, but I want to know what's on your mind."

I looked into his eyes. Eric seemed to be studying me.

"We *are* getting to know each other. This is me asking you out officially."

I blushed and nodded.

"It's settled." He leaned in and kissed me on the cheek. Then slowly his lips slid into a smile. "One more race?"

I stared at him for a moment, putting a hand to my cheek where his lips had touched.

I turned back to the wheel, and pressed *Start* again.

Chapter Ten

ERIC

My board lifted off the end of the half-pipe. This was it. My final trick would win the competition and secure my next pro contract. I completed the motions but, on the way down, my weight shifted. With no time to course-correct, I crashed to the ground.

I yelled out, jerking to a seated position in bed. Yanking back the covers, I checked my knee. It was scarred from the surgery but intact. I stumbled out of bed and rushed to the balcony. Sliding the door open, I stepped out into the cold and sucked in breath after breath.

It never felt like enough.

What was happening? I hadn't had a dream about my knee in months. I thought I finally had control of it. I tried daily to erase that moment from my mind. Not only because of the injury, but because it was the moment my dream ended and my future was changed forever.

I rubbed my thumb across the scar on my forehead almost unconsciously. I had to get out of my apartment.

I stepped back inside and grabbed my phone. I scrolled and found the number.

"Hello?"

"Hey. It's Eric. Can you do something today? I... I have to get out of here." My voice quavered.

"Sure. I know just the thing."

I arrived at the recreation center an hour later. Several guys and a couple women were spread out on a soccer field, throwing a Frisbee around. Lewis jumped up and made a catch before spotting me and jogging over.

"Hey! Glad you could make it," Lewis said. "This is my Ultimate Frisbee group. We play about twice a month. You're welcome anytime."

One guy tossed the Frisbee to another player and a guy on the other team jumped up to knock it away. The offensive team managed to catch it even as members of the opposing team collided with him. Hard. My stomach sank.

"Is this contact?" I asked Lewis.

"Technically, no. It's not football, but there is always the possibility of some contact. Just try to keep it clean."

One of the women dashed down the field for the Frisbee but was knocked down. She brushed it off and kept playing.

This was more than I expected. I was still rattled by my dream this morning. I could still jog and do basic exercises, but I would have no control over what happened on the field. Lewis didn't know about my knee, so he also didn't know what a bad idea this was. Regardless, I was tired of being held back by my injuries.

"Okay, I'm in. Let me stretch first."

My physical therapist taught me the importance of stretching. Even though I couldn't go back to snowboarding, I was fascinated by how the muscles that were not permanently damaged could recover.

"Whatever you need to do," Lewis called to me over his shoulder, rejoining his teammates on the field. "We'll get you in shortly, when we start a new match."

I took my time stretching out my legs and arms, making sure to concentrate. By the time I was ready, Lewis returned with the team.

He introduced me to everyone and gave me a quick rundown of the rules: The Frisbee is passed down the field from person to person only by throwing it. The player in possession cannot move from their position; they can only pivot in place to make the next pass. The rest of the team runs downfield, trying to be open for the next pass until they score in the end zone.

I ended up on a team with Lewis and learned everyone's names. We jogged to our side of the field, preparing to throw. We talked briefly about who we would guard. Finally, it was time for the game to begin. A guy named Ben threw the Frisbee, and we sprinted down the field to defend.

At first, everyone seemed to be finding their footing. The other team scored a point, but our team came right back and scored. After what felt like endless sprints up and down the field, we managed to intercept a throw and scored to get ahead.

Josh, one of my teammates, offered me the Frisbee to throw in at the end of a point. I grabbed it and got in position. I stepped forward, and my knee twinged, a warning to be cautious. I tossed the Frisbee and we charged down the field.

After each team scored a few more points, we neared the end of the match. We only needed one more point to win the game. I could feel soreness in my knee, but there was no stopping now. I pressed on, ignoring it. I wanted my old self back. I wanted to finish the match.

Josh made a pass to Lewis, who now stood a couple of feet away from me.

"Eric! Go long!"

I dashed downfield with a defender at my side. The Frisbee sliced through the air, higher than my reach. I jumped and, stretching my arm as high as I could, grabbed the Frisbee as the defender knocked into me. I crash-landed on my bad leg.

"Sorry, man," the guy said, offering a hand. When he saw my grimace, he retracted his hand and called out, "He's hurt!"

I gently pressed my leg and knee to gauge the extent of the injury. It hurt, but thankfully nothing felt torn. I hoped it was only sore. I would make a doctor's appointment to get it checked regardless.

Lewis hovered over me. "Are you okay?"

"Yes and no. My knee's messed up from an old injury. I thought I could play on it but turns out the last jump did me in. Can you help me up?"

"Yeah, of course."

I struggled up onto my good leg and wrapped my arm around Lewis's shoulder. He helped me off the field to a nearby bench.

"Man, we could have done something else if I knew."

"No, I wanted to play, and I didn't tell you. I thought maybe my body could handle it. I guess not."

He handed me a cold bottle of water from a nearby cooler, and I pressed it to my knee.

A cheer came from the field.

Lewis held out his hand. "Come on, it looks like our team won. Want to grab a victory drink and get some ice for that knee?"

I grabbed his hand and stood up. "Sounds good."

We ended up at Walko Taco, a bar downtown that served street tacos and a wide selection of beers on draft. We took a booth, where I was able to stretch out my leg. Lewis called a server over and asked for a bag of ice.

"This is my first time here," I told Lewis, glancing down at the menu.

"The best option is to pick a bunch of tacos with whatever meat you want. They're small, so I get several."

Our server returned with a bag of ice and took our orders as my stomach grumbled.

"So, what's the story with your knee?" Lewis asked.

"I had a pretty gnarly injury two years ago. I didn't land my snowboarding trick."

"Oh, wow. My bad for inviting you to Frisbee."

"No, if you had chosen to do something different because of my knee, that would have been worse. I can work out, and run some, but I have to be careful. Too much can strain it. It was a long recovery."

"I gotcha. Snowboarding, huh? You didn't grow up here?"

"No, my mom is originally from here, and we have family close by. I grew up in Colorado and started snowboarding when I was a kid. It's all I've ever known." I gritted my teeth. It was the last thing I wanted to talk about.

"Look, I get it. I put everything into opening Button Mashers. If something happened and I lost it, I don't know what I would do."

I nodded.

"So, what do you do for work?" Lewis asked.

I told him the same thing I told Jenna: "I'm a freelance video editor."

I hated lying. But the more people who knew, the more likely I would have to reveal my identity to everyone. The number of subs was ticking up on my reveal goal, and I was increasingly worried that I would have to show myself.

"That's cool. Man, I wish I had a skill like that. What type of videos do you edit?"

"It varies. I've done some editing for small business in the tech industry." Lies, lies, lies! Technically streaming was a small business—the business was you and your brand.

"That's great." Watching the bartenders serve some women drinks and tacos, Lewis took a sip of his beer. "Actually, if you need more work, maybe you could help me with a promo video for Button Mashers."

"Yeah, maybe I could do that." I hesitated. "I wouldn't want to mess anything up for you."

Lewis leaned back in his chair and crossed his arms. "Anything would help these days. I know the bar looks busy, but I'm always trying to figure out ways to expand. Take food, for example. I really want to add something other than bowls of mixed nuts, but that means outfitting the back room. The hookups are all there, but getting a cook, the equipment, and everything to code, well, it's not a cheap venture."

"What do you plan to do in the meantime?"

"Make good beer and sell it."

"Aren't you already?"

"Sure, but there are a lot of good places downtown. I don't want to be just another stop on the bar crawl. I want to be *the* stop, a destination. A place where people feel comfortable parking themselves all night for a good time."

"I don't know. It's the place where I want to be right now."

Lewis chucked. "I wonder why."

"That's part of it, but I do think it's pretty great—atmosphere, beer... owner."

"Thanks. At least you think so."

I took a sip of my beer. "What about you? You're getting phone numbers left and right but no woman has piqued your interest?"

Lewis shook his head. "I spend ninety percent of my time either at the bar or thinking about the business. My apartment is above the bar. I want to meet someone to spend my life with, but I don't see how that can happen right now. That woman would really have to be special."

"I get it. My work keeps me busy. Going to Button Mashers was out of the norm for me. If it's any encouragement, I think you could do it. Succeed *and* meet someone. Don't just hide away in the bar like Jenna."

Lewis froze. "What?"

"Nothing. I said nothing." I shoved a taco in my mouth.

"I knew you could tell she was Jenson. Does she know?"

"No, not yet. Please. I need time."

"Okay. Just don't take too long to level with her. She wouldn't want to be tricked like that."

"I'm not tricking her." I wasn't, was I? I didn't tell her I was EHucker. No. This was a separate issue. I couldn't tell anyone who I was. "I understand, though, why she hides. I hope I can help her get past it."

Lewis's eyes bugged out. "She told you the reason?"

I drew back. "You don't know?"

"No. I got the feeling she's been hurt, but she's never told me details."

"Sorry. I can't tell you if she hasn't told you."

"Agreed. That's for her to say. I'm glad she's opened up to someone. I think that's a big step. Don't take what she told you lightly."

"I won't."

We finished our tacos and drinks, chatting about sports and other light topics. It was interesting that even Lewis didn't know about the video. He was someone she seemed to trust, so if she didn't tell him, then what did that say about her trusting me?

Chapter Eleven

JENNA

Three days had passed since I made the bet with EHucker, and I hadn't heard from him. I watched him stream in the evenings. I didn't mind that he hadn't reached out. I was busy working and practicing for the next Button Mashers competition.

His stream last night went significantly long. He had already been live for three hours when I hopped on. As I watched, I grew more curious. He generally stuck to gaming topics, but every once in a while, he shared a nugget about his life. I knew he lived alone, had a sister, and enjoyed spicy foods. He'd avoided answering questions about his identity and anonymity until last night.

Several viewers started chatting about Darza, another well-known streamer. Darza had done well for himself and received many extra perks and much attention for his content. The chat asked EHucker why he didn't tell people who he was so he could get more recognition and participate in live interviews, sponsorships, and events.

EHucker pointed to the sub count at the top of his screen. "We have a goal to reach if we want face cam. Darza is a good guy, and more power to him for grinding and building his platform. I'm thankful for all the success my stream has had. And I'm thankful for all of you, my viewers. I wake up every day and stream because of you."

Some of the chat theorized that he was a celebrity, or they bashed him for just wanting more money. I pinched my lips together. Everyone who reached the point of streaming full time had worked hard to get there. The business of streaming relied on others who supported you and your content. Whatever reasons he had for making the goal, it helped.

I gifted five subs to his community.

"Thank you, Jenson, for those subs. Those indeed get us closer to the goal." Not many would catch it, but it sounded like his voice wavered when he mentioned the goal.

Several others gifted subs, and I watched the numbers in the top corner climb. The subs continued pouring in, and with each one EHucker thanked the person gifting it, but each thank-you became less and less enthusiastic.

"Okay, okay, let's get back to the game," he said, and soon the numbers slowed down.

He was an anomaly; it seemed like he wanted less attention, not more. Though he had set a seemingly unreachable goal, it looked like he could possibly reach it.

Now, taking a break from gaming, I was curled up on my couch watching *Ratatouille*. EHucker was offline, and there were no other streamers I wanted to watch. My phone lit up with a message on Discord.

I snatched my phone and opened the app to see a photo of *Ms. Pac-Man*'s screen with a high score listed under EHucker. I smiled and brought the phone close, squinting at the screen. I didn't recognize this place. It looked like he was in some sort of fun zone or children's arcade.

Another message came in.

EHucker360: So what's your secret?

Jenson: I haven't sent my score! How do I know this isn't doctored?

EHucker360: Ah, I thought that might be a problem.

After a few minutes, a video message came through. A cute kid appeared and said, "Hi Jenson. I'm Marcus. I watched your friend EHucker get the highest score on *Ms. Pac-Man*. Okay, bye!" There was some rustling. Then I thought I heard a voice different from the modified one from his stream say "Thanks, kid" before the screen went black. I played it again, listening to the quiet voice. I couldn't hear well but was able to confirm that I was definitely talking to a guy.

Jenson: You got a kid as your witness?

EHucker360: Yeah. He was more than happy to help once I gave him a ton of tokens.

I laughed that he bribed a kid to substantiate his claim. And if he was handing out tokens, he was at a kids' arcade.

Jenson: Unbelievable.

EHucker360: Well Jenson, get cracking on Ms. Pac-Man. *We didn't set up a time parameter. What do you say, a week to try to beat me before you concede? There's no way I'm streaming* Puppy Paws Adventure.

Jenson: Give me an hour.

I checked the time and sprung up from the couch. *Ratatouille* would have to wait. I changed from my cozy joggers to jeans and was out the door in no time. I wasn't going to let EHucker tease me and gloat for a week.

Twenty minutes later, I flew through the doors at Button Mashers. Lewis waved at me as I sped past him.

Yes! The *Ms. Pac-Man* machine was clear. I double-checked the score he sent me and tucked my phone into my pocket. No problem. I hit the *Start* button and began the game.

Two hours later, I collapsed on my couch back home. My tea sat cold on the coffee table, and the movie was no longer playing.

I grinned. EHucker had messaged me! And tonight was a success.

I pulled up the picture of my score and a video of Lewis vouching for me, and sent them both to EHucker.

EHucker360: I'm speechless.

Jenson: That blown away by my score? Ever seen such high numbers?

EHucker360: It's been over an hour.

Jenson: It took time to get there. Plus, you originally planned on giving me a week.

EHucker360: I'm embarrassed to say it took me five hours to get my score.

Jenson: Five hours! Do you want to go back and try to beat mine?

EHucker360: Unfortunately, I don't have another five hours to spare and anyway, I think I met my match. Well done, Jenson.

I beamed with pride. I honestly thought he would take the opportunity to better my score, but he seemed okay with accepting defeat. Which meant that he would be streaming *Puppy Paws Adventure*. I giggled.

Jenson: When do you think you'll stream Puppy Paws? *I want to be around when you do it.*

EHucker360: What are you doing now?

Jenson: Sitting on my couch. I was watching old Pixar movies before you messaged me tonight.

EHucker360: Well, load up Simmerz. I'll stream Puppy Paws Adventure *now.*

Jenson: Okay.

EHucker360: Before I start, did you challenge someone to a game?

Jenson: Ah yes, I challenged a guy I just started dating. Does that count?

EHucker360: I would say so. Did you win?

Jenson: Haha, no. But I had fun!

EHucker360: Glad to hear it. Starting now.

Moments later I received a notification that EHucker360 was going live. His stream title was "Special Stream: I lost a bet..." Under the game title, he had *Puppy Paws Adventure*.

When I clicked on it, his chat was already going nuts, asking him about the bet. He explained how he bet someone he could beat her at an arcade game, but lost. Some people made rude comments about him *"losing to a girl."* But overall, everyone was delighted. I expected to be more upset by the harsh comments, but the positivity seemed to dampen those, and soon I was laughing harder than I had in weeks.

As EHucker played through the game, he received more gifted subs. He thanked people for the subs, but I couldn't help but feel like every time, something seemed off about his responses. Regardless, it was fun to watch a grown man engage in a sweet game for little girls.

After his quick, easy game made for kids, he switched over to *Total Command* and continued streaming. When he took a break, I received a message.

EHucker360: I still want a secret.

Jenson: Hmm. I'll think about it. You did not win this bet. How about I share something about myself if you do?

I waited, watching his chat talking to each other. Some of the people were longtime subscribers, possibly friends. They knew things about each other's lives and asked intentional questions. Eric mentioned something about there being supportive communities online. Maybe this was what he was referring to, the ones who kept coming back and stayed.

My Discord chimed with an incoming message.

EHucker360: Streaming anonymously is like living two separate lives. I am who I am, but it's not the same. It's me the streamer versus me the regular guy. There are expectations and perceptions of what people think of me. It's exhausting sometimes.

Jenson: Then why do it?

EHucker360: A lot of reasons. Some I'm not ready to share. I've built a good community. I think even if streaming can be self-serving, people also need each other. Besides, even the chat at the end of the day is anonymous. I'm merely the vehicle through which they can connect.

Jenson: I think it's more than that. You are special, and people can see that. Not everyone can bring people together as you have. There is a lot to be said about that.

He didn't respond for a couple of minutes. I checked the stream, but he still had his *Be Right Back* screen up.

EHucker360: Thank you. That means a lot. Lately I've been wondering why I've continued streaming. Then I met you, and I feel like things have changed. I've changed. I don't know. I can't explain it.

I sucked in a breath. He shared more with me than I thought he would. I couldn't have possibly impacted him that much in our few interactions. On some level, though, I understood. There was an unexplainable connection between us.

It seemed silly to care for someone online, but I couldn't help how I felt. Gaming with EHucker brought back some of the joy I felt when I originally started gaming. Except it was different. I looked forward to any bits and pieces he shared with me.

Jenson: I understand.

EHucker360: I have to get back to the stream. Tell me your secret next time. I'll talk to you later, okay?

Jenson: Okay.

I watched his stream as long as I could until my eyes grew heavy, and I drifted off to sleep.

Chapter Twelve

ERIC

"You look beat," Emily said as we sat down at the diner for breakfast. I had forgotten about our plans until right before bed. One more game turned into five, and before I knew it, it was two hours later.

"I streamed until three a.m."

Emily narrowed her eyes. "Did you forget about me?"

"Never. You know how it is." I glanced around and combed my fingers through my hair. It was still damp from my shower.

"Actually no, I don't know how it is. I mean, I watch you sometimes, but I know you don't want me in your business. Also, I sleep and dance, that's it. I don't have a lot of extra time. And you don't ever talk about what you do."

"You guys don't like it."

"Mom doesn't like it. I support you, and I think Dad doesn't care either way as long as you're taking care of yourself. Which I don't believe you are. Physically yes. Mentally, I'm not so sure."

I huffed. "Why would you say that?"

"Because you're always distracted, and I've noticed you've become increasingly distant since we moved here. Yes, we hang out, but it's not the same as before."

"Coffee?" the server asked.

Thankful for the interruption, I ordered a black coffee and a veggie omelet. My sister also ordered a coffee and a waffle. In no time the waitress returned with two mugs and a pot of coffee. She sat down the cups and filled them both. I almost wished the woman would leave the whole coffee pot on the table. It was going to be that sort of day.

My phone buzzed. When I glanced at it, my heart fluttered. It was Jenson. I swiped my thumb to open the message but stopped when Emily said, "Who's that?"

"No one," I said, slipping my phone back into my pocket.

"Oh! Was it Jenna?" Emily clapped her hands in excitement.

"No, a gamer friend."

Emily rolled her eyes. "Of course."

"Anyway, I wanted to apologize."

"For what?"

"For acting like a jerk about the whole Justin thing."

"It's cool. It wasn't right for me to bring it up in front of Jenna. We just worry about you."

"I know. I'm fine." At least I wanted it to be. I took a sip of my coffee as Emily caught me up on her week.

After a bit, the waitress returned with our food. Emily doused her waffle with syrup and I added hot sauce to my omelet.

"I know you don't want to talk about it," she began, "but I was cracking up at you playing *Puppy Paws Adventure!*"

"You watched that?"

"Yeah. I saw your stream notification and did a double take. It makes sense it was a bet." She raised her eyebrows. "Did the gamer friend who texted you make the bet?"

I nodded. I couldn't help the small smile as I picked up my crispy, hot bacon and took a bite.

"Wait, is your gamer friend a woman? Is it Jenna?"

Nothing got by Em, but I couldn't admit Jenson was indeed Jenna. In my mind, her in real life and her online were separate identities. It only helped me feel less guilty about masking myself as EHucker.

"No, it's not her," I lied.

"But I like Jenna. For once I like who you're seeing. Don't mess it up with her."

"As I said, she's a friend. No worries. I like Jenna too. I'll try to not mess it up," I told Emily not as confidently as I'd hoped. I already feared I was messing it up, though she did agree to a date. And I knew the perfect place to take her.

We continued chatting and eating. I itched to read my message from Jenson, but I didn't want Emily to ask me any more questions.

Finally, we finished our food, and I paid the bill. Emily's friends picked her up, and I slipped into my car. At last, I could read the Discord message.

Jenson: A secret. You're the first person I've used a mic with while gaming in years. You've helped me too. I've been lonely, but now I'm not. Thank you.

I understood exactly what she meant.

Back in my apartment, I dropped my keys on the counter and kicked off my boots. I was met by silence. I grabbed the TV remote and flipped through the channels. As usual, nothing was on.

I turned on my Xbox and booted up Simmerz. Trekster was streaming, so I put it on for background noise.

My phone buzzed in my pocket. Excited about the prospect of it being Jenson/Jenna, I pulled it out quickly. It was Justin. I clicked the *Ignore* button and tossed my phone on the couch.

Why wouldn't he leave me alone? I didn't want to remember.

Frustrated, I stood from the couch only to have my bum knee throb again from the Ultimate Frisbee injury. Thankfully the urgent care doctor said it would be fine. I would have to do extra stretches to ensure it didn't get worse.

I tried to push Justin out of my mind. A constant reminder. A constant feeling of loss I could never escape.

Suddenly, I felt it. My chest tightened. My mind screamed at me to do something. Quick. I paced around the room, trying to shut down the thoughts. I never forgot. I never said goodbye to Justin. I just left.

Now I have my stream. It would get me out of this mess. If only I did enough, made enough, streamed enough, I could pay everyone back. I tried to reassure myself, but there was no comfort at a dead-end.

The air in my apartment grew thicker and warmer. It was too hot, too suffocating. I bent over, hands on my knees.

So difficult to breathe.

I forced myself into the kitchen, stumbling, and filled a glass of water, taking small sips, trying to regulate my breathing. I couldn't participate in sports anymore, but there was no way I was this out of shape.

Why was this happening?

Recovering from the injury was taxing my body. That had to be it. I needed to relax.

I took a step outside and took some deep breaths of the cold air. I stared at the street below, watching the cars pass by. Slowly, my chest loosened and I didn't think about the past.

I went back inside and plopped down on the couch again to watch Trekster play a new shooter game, trying to refocus. I hadn't played it before, and it seemed fun. Maybe I would include it on my stream next week.

Eventually I drifted to sleep to Trekster talking to his chat and the sound of online gunshots.

I woke up yelling, and dripping with sweat. I checked my arms and legs: still intact.

I was still here.

Chapter Thirteen

JENNA

"Ugh!" I cried as I threw another outfit on my bed. The pile of discarded clothes was mountain high. I couldn't figure out what to wear on my date with Eric. I texted him for hints of what we'd be doing, but all he said was to wear something I could move in.

What was I supposed to glean from that? Were we playing tennis or hiking up a rocky slope? I wanted to look nice, but I hadn't been out on a date in ages. When I was dating Thomas, he never noticed what I wore, so I dressed casually. After we became a couple, our dates were ordinary, just hangouts retitled as dates.

I vetoed another outfit when the doorbell rang. Pulling the curtain aside, I saw Alyssa bouncing on her toes. I hurried to the front door and swung it open.

"I'm engaged!" Alyssa danced through the doorway, threw her arms around me, and spun us both around.

"Congratulations! He finally asked you." We cheered and jumped up and down together. Finally, we stepped back, and I grabbed her hand and inspected the ring I had already seen. It came alive on her hand, like she was in a Zales commercial. "So beautiful. Come on, tell me about his proposal as you help me pick out an outfit."

Alyssa followed me to my room and flopped down on my messy bed while I peered into the closet once more.

"It was perfect!" she gushed. "Last night Bryan took me ice-skating even though he's terrible at it. We skated slowly around the rink a few times, holding hands, until he told me to take a lap without him." She gazed down at her ring and smiled. "Well, I circled the rink to find he had fallen, so, of course, I rushed over to him."

"Of course."

Alyssa clasped her hands to her chest and looked dreamily toward the ceiling. "I held out my hands to help him up, but he put a hand up to stop me. He managed to pop one skate up on the ice, so he was kneeling. Then he pulled out the ring and asked me!"

"I'm so happy for you. And I don't have to secretly divert your attention anymore."

"What? You knew?"

I flipped through some more shirts. "He only confided that he wanted to. I didn't know the when or how."

"Well, he surprised me all right."

"It's funny he used his fall as the perfect moment."

The two of us laughed.

"I know, right? Jenna, I'm so excited to marry him. I love him so much."

I smiled. I was thrilled that my two best friends would be joined together forever. I hoped to find someone who was my perfect match someday. I held up a navy blouse. I wasn't looking for anyone at the moment, not with SimmerzCon on the horizon, but here I was going on a first date. You never knew.

"Go with a dress," Alyssa said, interrupting my thoughts. She pulled out a tight red dress that would hug all my curves.

I wrinkled my nose. "Where did that come from?"

"I may have snuck it in the back of your closet last week."

"I cannot wear that. And besides, he said I need to be able to move."

Alyssa rolled her eyes and stuck the dress back in my closet. "Fine. What about this?" She held up a knee-length black dress with a high neckline. I opened my mouth to protest. "With tights and flat booties."

"That could work."

I slipped it on and looked in the mirror. It was perfect. I felt pretty, and I could move freely.

"Come here, let me do your hair." Alyssa patted the seat of the chair. She warmed up the curling iron and got to work on some simple, soft curls. "So what is the latest with your internet friend?"

"Well, while we were at Button Mashers, he messaged me and made a bet that he could get a higher score on *Ms. Pac-Man.*"

"Who won?"

"I did," I said with a smile. "Then he had to stream a Puppy Paws game. That was what I bet him. It was hilarious."

I didn't tell Alyssa what he shared with me.

"Do you think you'll play with him again?"

"I don't know. He seems nice enough. I just always get caught up in the what-if. What if I'm turned into another internet joke?"

Alyssa added the last loose curl to my hair and fluffed it along with all the other waves, then she sighed. "You were worried about the same thing meeting Eric, and look where you are. About to go on a date with a really great guy. EHucker could be an awesome friend to play games with. You won't know if you don't try. Maybe it will give you confidence to play at Button Mashers as *you.*"

Alyssa knew me. She didn't always understand my passion for gaming, but she understood that the MyVid video stole my light. Yes, she made fun of my Button Mashers disguise, but that was because Alyssa knew this was an over-reaction to what happened with Thomas. I used to be a very confident person especially when it came to video games.

Alyssa grabbed my cosmetics bag. "Time to do your makeup." She rummaged through it then held out a tube of red lipstick.

"Red? Did you plant that too?"

"Yes, red. It's a deep red that'll stand out with your black dress and still look classy."

"Fine."

She quietly worked on my makeup and, when she was done,

spun me around to face the mirror. I looked… hot. It was more than my daily look, yet it was still, for the most part, subtle. The eyeliner made my brown eyes pop, and the red lips highlighted my white teeth."

"Thanks, Alyssa."

She beamed. "Anytime."

The doorbell rang.

"I got it!" Alyssa announced, jumping up from the bed. "I want to see his face when you step into the room." She winked and ran to the door.

"Alyssa?" he said. "Is Jenna here? I'm taking her out tonight."

"Hey, Eric. She'll be out in a second. So… what are your intentions with my friend tonight?"

"Uh…"

"Okay, Alyssa. Time for you to go," I said with a laugh as I stepped into the foyer.

"Wow. Jenna. You look beautiful." He stared at me, Alyssa forgotten.

His hands were jammed into the pockets of his dark jeans. He wore a plaid button-up and his signature beanie hat.

"Did I overdress?" I asked, eyeing his outfit.

"No. Leave that on. Please."

I blushed and Alyssa looked between the two of us, a wide smile on her face. "Well, my job is done. Call me tomorrow, Jenna." Alyssa pranced out the door, singing, "Love is in the air."

Eric watched her go. "She's happy."

"Yeah, Bryan proposed. She's high on love right now."

He nodded. "Shall we go?"

"Yeah, but seriously, is this outfit okay for what we're doing?"

"You'll be fine," he said, looking at my shoes. "You're going to love it."

Ten minutes later, we pulled up to our destination.

"Laser tag!" I squealed, clapping my hands. "I haven't been

here in ages." I jumped out of the car and marched toward the entrance. Eric jogged to catch up with me. He took my hand, slowing me down.

"I'm glad you like it."

"I love it."

He gave me one of those rare smiles of his. We entered the building and paid for a match. We were put in a group of kids, the oldest of which were two boys who looked like middle schoolers. Several eyed us like we were too old to play.

"It said all ages on the website, but I didn't expect so many kids," Eric whispered.

"Adults probably come in later. Don't worry. This is great. We're going to crush them."

Eric chuckled, presumably at the competitive glint in my eye.

A teenage worker appeared, introduced himself, and explained the rules and how the vests and phasers worked. He instructed us to split up into teams.

"What do you want to do? Be on the same team and take all these kids down or go against each other?" Eric asked.

"I'd like to stack my victories against you. First *Space Invaders*, now this. Let's join opposite teams."

"Sounds good, beautiful. But no more victories for you." Eric winked.

My heart fluttered, and for a moment I forgot about the game.

"Yo, lady. You with us?" one of the middle schoolers asked.

"Sure." I glanced at Eric one last time. He'd already joined the red team. I faced the kids in front of me. "All right. Here's what we should do."

Chapter Fourteen

ERIC

"Not again," I groaned. Kids swarmed the arena, but it wasn't them I was worried about. It was the laser ninja in the black dress. My vest had lit up for what felt like the tenth time by Jenna's hand. We tagged the other kids as we came across them, but they were mostly focused on their friends. Meanwhile, Jenna and I were concentrating on each other. I tagged her several times; however, she was sneaky and fast. Our scores had to be close.

I peeked around the corner from the direction I was tagged to see a swoosh of black material disappearing behind a padded wall. Then she quickly spun past a gap to hide behind another object. I whistled low, impressed by her movement. Her outfit did not slow her down at all.

I glanced up at the clock. Two minutes remained in this final ten-minute round. I needed to act quickly to pull ahead.

I chanced one more look around my barrier and saw her peeking out down the lane. I pivoted and snuck the opposite way down the side, phaser at the ready. I tagged her in the back and hurried behind a wall before she turned around.

"Watch your back!" I teased, ducking my head as her phaser sounded. I took a peek, but she was already gone. I zigzagged past several objects and dashed to the next when my body collided with something small and soft.

"Ow!"

"I'm sorry." I grabbed Jenna's arms to steady her. The wall behind me prevented me from backing up. She leaned against me, our vests touching. "Are you okay?" I watched her face, worried I had hurt her.

"I'm okay."

I let go of her arms, giving her a chance to back away and find her footing again. Instead, she met my eyes then reached up and put her hand on my face. I looked at her red lips, which had been taunting me since I picked her up. She bit her lower lip, and I leaned in. But then, her eyes shifted and fixed on something behind me.

I felt pressure on the side of my vest. My eyes widened.

"Game over," she said, pressing the trigger, tagging me for the final point of the match.

My vest lit up, and the buzzer sounded. The blue team won, 45–44.

She stepped back, blew on the tip of her phaser, then ran to join her team in celebration.

"Good game," I told the kids on my team.

The tween stared at me.

"What?"

"Man, she had you." He laughed and walked away, joining his friend from the blue team.

I shook my head and returned my gear. When Jenna finished doling out high-fives, she sauntered over to me, elated.

"You play dirty," I said. "First, you grabbed my arm during *Space Invaders,* and now this."

"You ran into me, and you had a phaser in your hand too."

"You... distracted me."

She laughed. "Did I? Hmm. Oops, didn't mean to." She bit her lip again and looked away, trying to hide her obvious glee.

Another grin tugged at my mouth. I wasn't used to smiling this much. "You hungry?"

She replied with a nod.

"I know a great place."

"What is this madness?" I said as I entered the third roundabout in a row. I had taken a different route to avoid the highway, but that was a mistake.

Jenna giggled. "Did you not have roundabouts in Colorado?"

"Not sequentially. Maybe in the city somewhere, but in the mountains, my biggest concern was the ice, snow, and winding roads in the middle of winter. Even then, three roundabouts in a row? Seriously?"

These weren't roundabouts. We were literally completing figure eights in a car, trying to get out of a suburb of Indianapolis.

"They did go a bit overboard when they updated this road years ago."

Frowning, I exited what I hoped was the last one. Jenna seemed relaxed and happy. Funny, it felt like she always belonged in my passenger seat.

I cleared my throat. "If it's okay, I want to take you to my place for dinner."

"You cook?"

"A little. But if you'd rather go somewhere else, we can."

"No, your place sounds good. I'm excited."

I could hear the sincerity in her voice. I didn't normally cook on a first date, and it was a risk not knowing what she liked, but somehow, I knew she would prefer it over a fancy restaurant.

When we reached my apartment, I swiftly got out and came around the car to take her hand. We walked to my door, avoiding all the icy spots.

Once inside she kicked off her boots, and I took her coat. She scanned my apartment, then sniffed the air. "Oh, that smells good. Did you make something already?

"Chili in the slow cooker. It's my favorite thing to make on a cold day."

She laughed. "You rarely wear a coat. Is chili your secret to staying warm?"

I paused. I didn't realize she'd noticed. Or cared enough to say anything.

"Yeah. It's my mom's recipe. Give me a minute. Make yourself at home." I gestured to the living room couch then went to the kitchen and started pulling out salad ingredients and chili toppings.

I lined the ingredients out on the counter that faced the living room. My apartment was smaller and the kitchen and living room were right next to each other.

She didn't sit on the couch. Instead, she wandered about and stopped to study my film collection before moving on to the reading selection on my bookshelf. My place was nothing fancy. It held the things I needed to live and that's pretty much it.

"Is this Justin?"

"What?" I dropped the salad tongs then quickly picked them up and rinsed them off in the sink.

She held up a picture of Justin sitting in the snow, his snowboard beside him. He stared up into the camera. Emily must have snapped that picture.

"Where did you get that?"

"It was between these books."

"Oh." I cringed. I forgot I'd tucked it away when I moved. "Yeah, that's him." I added the tongs to the salad.

I expected her to ask more questions about Justin. Instead, she asked how Emily was doing.

"She's great. We had breakfast again. She picks our hangouts, so it could be anything. One time she made me shop for three hours with her. It wasn't bad until we got to the shoe store." I shuddered at the memory.

Jenna laughed. "There are a lot of women's shoes to choose from."

I hung my head. "I know this now." I took bowls out of the cabinet and set them on the kitchen counter. "Dinner is ready."

"Wow, that was fast." She crossed the room and took in the spread.

"I don't know how you like your chili, so help yourself."

She lifted out two bowls from the stack, one for salad and another for chili. I did the same and poured a glass of wine for each of us after asking what she liked. We sat at my small table just to the left of the kitchen.

"This is delicious," she said, scooping a large spoonful of chili into her mouth. When she finished chewing, she took a sip of wine, and the red lipstick stained the rim of the glass. I swallowed and glanced at her lips. They looked so soft. So…

I ran my hand through my hair and cleared my throat.

"I befriended one of those kids," said Jenna. "He was super on board with my plan of attack." She was talking about a one of the older kids at laser tag.

"I bet you did. He kept staring at you."

"He wasn't! He was a nice kid. Made me feel a part of the team."

"Trust me. I was a middle school boy once. He was crushing on you," I said.

She pinched her lips together. "Well, I didn't notice. I was too busy looking at someone else."

"And who might that be?"

She blushed. "Don't make me say it."

I just winked at her, and she laughed. I stabbed the lettuce of my salad and smiled.

"Laser tag was kind of the perfect date," said Jenna.

"I thought you might like it, since you seem to enjoy competition."

"What do you mean?" she asked.

"Well, between Button Masher tournaments, *Space Invaders*, and bowling, I figured laser tag was a safe bet."

"Button Masher tournaments..."

I froze, then: "Jenson, it's okay." I'd blurted out her gamertag without thinking.

Her eyes widened. "What did you just say?"

"Jenna. I said Jenna."

She slid her chair back and stood up. "No, you said Jenson. How? When?"

I thought she was angry at me, but when I looked into her eyes, all I saw was fear—the fear of being discovered. I felt that every day I was EHucker despite my ridiculous sub goal promise. Considering EHucker was the person who communicated with Jenson, I knew where her thoughts could lead.

"I knew the first night. When I saw you at Button Mashers. Your disguise, I saw through it."

"Can I... Where is your bathroom?"

I pointed down the hall. "First door on the right."

Too nervous to sit and wait, I grabbed our dishes and rinsed them in the sink. I put the lids back on all the topping containers and put them back in the fridge. I could only imagine what she was thinking. Was she mad or ready to run? She had to know I didn't care she was Jenson. I only wanted to know why.

She hadn't returned yet. Thoughts of her crying her eyes out in my bathroom while I casually put our dishes away had me striding down the hall. The bathroom door was open, I peeked my head in, but she wasn't there. My office door was still shut. I eyed my open bedroom at the end of the hall.

She stood by my bedside table, staring down at something in her hand. She turned it over. She was holding my lucky penny. I kept it in my pocket at every snowboarding event. It was one of those crushed pennies you got from a machine at a museum. This one was from a snowboarding museum in Washington state. My dad took me there when I was seven.

I leaned against the door, watching her. At least she wasn't in tears. After a few moments, I spoke. "Snooping?"

She jumped and set the penny back down.

"Sorry."

"Don't be," I told her, coming to stand in front of her.

I lifted her chin so she would meet my eyes. "Will you talk to me?"

I put her hand in mine and led her toward the living room. I looked back when she paused in the hall.

"What's this room?"

I panicked inside but managed to conceal it. She was looking at the door of my office.

"Just an extra room. Mostly boxes and things I haven't unpacked." I knew that I should tell her the truth, but when I thought about doing it, I felt sick to my stomach. I remembered why I chose to stream with the voice changer and no camera. Eventually this would go away when I stopped streaming and then it wouldn't matter. It would just be me and Jenna.

She seemed to accept my explanation as we made our way to the couch.

"Jenna, I'm sorry I didn't tell you right away. You seemed adamant about hiding who you were and I wanted to respect that."

She exhaled. "I'm not mad. I just needed a minute. I'm actually relieved that you know."

"Really?"

"I dress up as Jenson so no one notices I'm a woman. It's easier that way."

"Easier for who? You or the other guys?"

"Both. My brother, Matt, was into video games. We played *Mario Kart* together all the time and ever since then, gaming has been part of my life." She shook her head. "He died in a car accident when I was thirteen. He was four years older than me, but he was my best friend. Even if he had his friends over, he never treated me like an annoying sister."

I smiled a little. "So that's where your love of gaming comes from."

"Yeah. Even though it's been ten years, gaming helps me remember him."

"And you disguise yourself because of the *trained girl* video?"

She huffed out a laugh. "Basically. I don't want anyone to judge my gameplay because I'm a woman. If I make a mistake, no one can point and laugh and say I didn't have enough training from my ex. Yes, that did actually happen once when I was gaming with voice chat under my old gamertag. I want to be on equal ground. My ex has competed at SimmerzCon in the past. I'm guessing he'll be there again. If so, I plan to exact my revenge."

I raised an eyebrow. This was... alarming at best.

"What kind of revenge?" I asked carefully.

"I want to beat him at his own game. I'm going to show him that I can compete at a high level and that I'm over what he did to me."

I studied Jenna. This was not the woman I knew until this point. Her hurt ran a lot deeper than I even realized from our first conversation about gaming when we were bowling. It seemed like my efforts as EHucker weren't helping at all.

"Jenna, I have a confession."

She turned to me with a look of open curiosity.

"I watched the video. I know you asked me not to, but I had to know what you were facing. To be fair, I just watched part of it. I only needed a few minutes to get the gist."

"Oh," she said, her eyes now cast down to the floor.

"Your ex is an absolute idiot." I gently raised her chin so she would look in my eyes. "He is not worth one more second of worry. Not one more second of your thoughts. If you want to get into SimmerzCon, do it because you love to game, not because you have to prove anything to anyone. Compete for you and as you."

"But if I'm Jenson, I'm not bothering anyone. No one will think of me as someone that had to be trained to compete. Everyone's happy." She let out a strangled cry.

"Everyone, except *you*."

She looked down again. "One time I turned on my mic and I was immediately hit on and getting asked what I looked like when I was just trying to play the game. Recently a guy said my favorite game was a man's game. I think that hurt more."

I wanted to tell off anyone who ever made Jenna feel this way. It made me want to scream. I couldn't stop random comments, but I could help her see what was true.

I pulled her into my arms and spoke softly against her ear. "I'm sorry you had to go through that, Jenna. People say terrible things when they're hidden behind a screen name. They lash out because of their own insecurities. That's not on you. That's not for you to shoulder."

She sat back and turned to me.

"Thank you. I didn't know that was what I needed to hear until now. I am taking steps though. Remember when I mentioned that I played a game with that streamer? We played a few more times, and it was a lot of fun. He's a good guy. Maybe you know him? He goes by EHucker360."

When I didn't respond, she continued.

"Oh sorry, I forgot you aren't much of a gamer. You probably don't watch streamers. Or do you?"

I cringed internally and tried to shift the conversation back to her. "Jenna, compete in the next Button Masher's tournament as you. I'll be there for you, if anyone says anything."

"Like Carter?"

I clenched my fist. "Yes, I'll be there."

Our eyes met again.

"Jenna, I see *you*," I whispered, leaning in close.

Her eyes scanned my face, and suddenly her lips pressed to mine. I paused, shocked for a moment, but then I kissed her back.

Her kisses were light at first, maybe testing the waters a little bit, but then I pressed in and deepened the kiss. Ever since she stepped into the foyer when I picked her up, I wanted to bring her in close and kiss her. Now that it was happening, I never wanted to stop. All the things I worried about had disappeared. She drew my bottom lip between hers, and I weaved my fingers into her hair. I ran my tongue across her bottom lip. She pulled back abruptly, panting.

I inhaled deeply, trying to regain my bearings. This time the air I needed wasn't cold and empty. It was warm and satisfying, like the sun had come out after a long winter.

She reached out, brought her thumb to the corner of my mouth, and dragged it across the bottom edge.

"Lipstick." She smiled, the natural pink of her lips coming through.

"I'll keep it," I said, happy to have any part of her with me.

We decided to watch a movie before I took her home. After settling on *Ocean's Eleven*, I relaxed on the couch, breathing in her scent, my heart beating wildly. Alive.

I finally felt alive again.

Chapter Fifteen

JENNA

A few days after my date with Eric, what he said hit me: Why was I still letting that video bother me after all this time? Was I happy putting on a disguise every time I competed at Button Mashers?

I walked over to my bag and pulled out the oversize hoodie I wore to tournaments. I pulled it over my head and walked over to my mirror. It had no meaning or significance. I bought it in the men's section of a second-hand store with the sole intention of covering who I was. I thought I was doing a good job, yet Eric still saw me.

I opened MyVid to see if TakeNote had posted any new videos highlighting the best moments from her stream—I missed most of them now since I had been watching EHucker instead.

Then I scrolled through the site's suggested videos. My heart dropped to my stomach. *Trained girl* was trending again. Why in the world was it trending?

I told myself to move on and forget about it; nothing anyone said mattered. Unfortunately that wasn't enough to suppress my curiosity, and I clicked on the video to read the new comments.

There were a bunch of short insults, like *"trash," "lol she sux,"* and *"not your game."* And it escalated from there—blatantly demeaning to borderline threatening.

I kept scrolling, feeling sicker and sicker. Then the comments changed to questions: *"what?"* and *"where did it go?"*

I refreshed my browser, and the content was now unavailable. Did Thomas take it down? Or the MyVid administrator? The latter seemed more likely. Relief washed over me, then a mixture of joy and anger. I wiped the tears from my face, not realizing that I had been crying. The video brought me straight back to a collection of humiliating memories from when it was released.

I backed out of it and scrolled through the other suggested videos.

Trekster, a streamer EHucker sometimes played with, had posted something. A reaction video titled, *Trekster Reacts to Viral Gaming Moments.*

I clicked into it. I watched through the 30-second clips of takedowns in *Total Command* and the greatest tricks in *New Day* enjoying all the awesome moments in gaming. Until I saw it: a clip from the *trained girl* video. That had to be what caused its sudden resurgence.

Trekster scoffed at the clip and asked, "This guy went viral for *this?* Nah, bad content." Then the next clip played.

I was relieved at the way he reacted, but I still felt nauseated. This was exactly why I disguised myself, why I couldn't show anyone who I was.

I was going to play a couple of matches of *Total Command,* but now I didn't want to interact with anyone.

I made my way over to my closet and pulled out the box of Matt's things. I felt a pang in my heart as each item reminded me of him. He would have been twenty-seven years old now, maybe married or off in another country helping others. That was the kind of person he was.

I pulled out a copy of *Assassin's Creed,* one of the earlier games.

I installed it and waited for it to boot up. When it finally loaded, I stared at the screen for a full five minutes. This was the game he was playing before… before he was gone.

"Matt, come on!" I had said at the time. "You've been obsessed since you got this Xbox. Can't we play together on the N64?"

Matt paused his game and took a moment to look at me. I was laying on his bed, flipping through a magazine.

"Jenna, I promise when I'm done beating this game, we can play hours of N64."

"Hours?" I asked hopefully.

"Yes." He placed his fist over his heart, his sign to me that he would keep his promise.

I put my fist to my heart too.

He unpaused the game, and I watched him play through the story, waiting for the ending.

Now, sitting on the couch, I clutched my fist to my heart and started the game.

Accustomed to faster-paced games, I was lost and a bit bored after about an hour. I did not have the patience for a storyline adventure right now. I wanted to hop back into my favorite battle royale.

My phone dinged, and a message appeared on my Discord.

EHucker: Assassin's Creed? *Man, and an old one too.*

Under my name on Discord, he could see what game I was playing. I hesitated. EHucker probably saw the video too. I was curious what he thought. Either way, he didn't know it was me so what did it matter?

Jenson: Yeah. It was my brother's game.

EHucker: Was?

Jenson: It was the last game he played before he passed away.

EHucker: I'm sorry…

Jenson: It's okay.

EHucker: Do you want to talk about what prompted you to play it?

I sighed. I wondered if I could talk to him about what happened. Maybe not specifically but possibly in a roundabout way.

Jenson: Have you ever had someone post something about you that affected your real life?

He took a while to reply.

EHucker: Yes. Why? Did something happen to you?

Jenson: Yes. I had a video go viral about me while I was in school, and now it's resurfaced. It's embarrassing and hurtful. I want nothing more than to get back at the person who posted it.

When I told Eric on our date that I wanted revenge on my ex, I thought how ridiculous it sounded out loud. But now it didn't seem too wild to feel that way. If Thomas was the one who took it down, then why? It had been available for years. Could he have changed somehow?

EHucker: Then get back at that person. Make them pay.

All I could do was blink. This was a vastly different reaction than Eric's. The chat bubble appeared again.

EHucker: After you make them pay, all will be forgiven, right? You'll feel better?

Jenson: Well, no.

EHucker: Then why choose revenge?

Dang. He got me too. Like Eric, he was making me doubt myself.

Jenson: You don't understand. You probably liked the video your buddy Trekster watched. You probably laughed.

EHucker: The video Trekster watched? What are you talking about?

Jenson: His reaction video. There's one clip in there from the video I'm talking about.

It was quiet for a while, so I figured I'd made him mad. If I was honest, I didn't know what I was doing. EHucker had nothing to do with it, but I was taking my anger out on him. I got up and started unloading the dishwasher. When I finished, I checked my phone and found a flurry of messages.

EHucker: I think I know which clip you mean.

EHucker: I'm sorry. I didn't realize he commented on that.

EHucker: It's a terrible clip. How could that person do that?

EHucker: Jenson? That clip just makes me mad.

EHucker: Jenson?

I quickly started typing.

Jenson: I guess it's irrelevant now. Someone took the video down.

EHucker: Yeah.

Jenson: I'm sorry for reacting like that. You have to understand that this video has haunted me for a long time. And now that it's resurfaced, it's going to be a nightmare, just like it was years ago.

EHucker: What was it like?

I thought back to all the looks and whispers on campus. I recalled how Thomas got internet famous, praised for the laughs. It only inflated his ego.

Jenson: Horrible. It destroyed my perception of gaming. It distracted me from my classes. I was a laughingstock on campus. I almost dropped out, but my friends kept me going.

EHucker: I'll tell Trekster to take the video down.

Jenson: No, please. It's just one clip. He had no idea. Don't make it a big deal. He's a content creator. It's how he makes money.

EHucker: I'll make a new video with him. Or at least edit the video and repost it.

I didn't know what to say about that. I didn't mean to get anyone involved in my drama. Now I felt bad. I wanted to disappear.

EHucker: The things people say on the internet mean nothing. There are so many videos that come out now, this will fade out as fast as it came.

He was right. Each year it felt like people were more and more distracted with what they saw online that they soon forgot and would move on to the next thing, leaving their harsh comments that hurt someone behind.

Jenson: I suppose you would know about that.

Since I started watching his stream, I had seen him ignore the onslaught of criticism thrown his way. Even if he never reacted to it, it must have grated on his nerves from time to time.

EHucker: Yeah. Unfortunately I do.

I wanted to ask him more, but he started typing again.

EHucker: Do you feel like playing a couple games of Total Command? *It'll be easier to talk.*

After playing an hour of *Assassin's Creed*, I was ready to return to my favorite game. And playing with EHucker felt safe.

Jenson: Sure.

I booted up the game and put on my headset. He invited me to his lobby, and we said hello. We both pressed *Ready* and waited for the action to start.

We didn't talk about anything personal, just commentary on the game. After several matches, we returned to the lobby.

"Were you going to stream tonight?" I asked.

"No. I have a lot on my mind."

"Do you want to talk about it?"

He was quiet for a couple of minutes. I started to wonder if he was still there.

"There's nothing in particular that happened. I just get tired of entertaining my chat sometimes."

"I don't think you have to entertain anyone. They're there because they enjoy listening to you and watching you play. You only have to be yourself and people will stay."

"Or they're there out of morbid curiosity."

"Maybe. Does it matter? You know Simmerz chat is flippant. Your true followers will stay no matter what."

He paused. "Will you stay, Jenson?"

Even with the voice changer, I could hear the emotion in his voice, and it caught me off guard. "What do you mean?"

"Will you stay? If I never streamed again? If you knew who I was, would you stay?"

I furrowed my brows. He had a goal to eventually reveal himself. Though every time I saw people donate, he seemed thankful but wary. Whatever this was about, EHucker was someone I'd looked forward to talking with, so to think he could just disappear...

I never considered that.

"I would stay. Are you okay?" I asked.

He laughed. "Yeah, Jenson. Everything is okay. Look, I need to go."

"Oh, okay," I said, startled by his abrupt departure.

"I'd love to talk to you all night, but I have an early stream with Trekster."

I glanced at the clock. Shoot, it was 1 a.m., and I had a morning shift at the coffee shop. I was going to need a whole pot of coffee tomorrow.

"I didn't realize the time," I said.

"Me either."

"Hucker? Before you go, I want you to know that I don't care who you are. I mean, I care and I..." Catching myself, I trailed off.

"You what?"

"I want to stay. I need to. Please, stay too."

"I will, Jenson. For you, I will."

He logged off, and I sat there. I reached up to brush a tear away. Everything had hit me at once. The video being reposted, missing Matt, and talking to EHucker. I was still trying to figure him out. I don't know why he had the goal for a face cam when he seemed so against it.

Regardless, if I ever found out who he was or not, I knew one thing: I wasn't going anywhere.

Chapter Sixteen

ERIC

Forcing my eyes open, I crawled out of bed the next morning at dawn. I was running on five hours of sleep after tossing and turning for a solid hour last night. I was starting to regret agreeing to an early stream with Trekster.

A moment of insanity. That's the only thing that could explain it.

Thankfully I had enough sense last night to set the coffeemaker to autostart, and the smell of freshly brewed coffee hit my nose as soon as I opened the bedroom door. I made my way to the kitchen and poured myself a cup. Black as tar, thank you.

After a few sips, I stretched and did my exercises. Ever since the scare at Ultimate Frisbee, I was careful to do them every day.

Once I was done, I grabbed my mug and stepped out onto the balcony. I welcomed the cold under my feet and a crisp breeze across my bare chest. I sipped my coffee, which warmed my insides. I was in no rush. The benefit of streaming without a camera was not needing to look presentable for viewers.

I leaned on the balcony. The snow was no longer fresh, and cars were caked with dirt from the beat-up snow. I missed the pristine snow of the Colorado mountains. As I would get ready to tip my board over the edge, there was nothing like it. I felt free gliding down into the white expanse. Here it was all flat, and I didn't feel free at all. I felt like all my messiness was on display for everyone to walk all over.

My phone buzzed with a text.

Jenna: Good morning, Eric. Did you see?

I stared at the text. What did I miss? I clicked on MyVid, but nothing else had posted. I pinched the bridge of my nose, took a deep breath, and played dumb.

Eric: Good morning. No, what are you talking about?

Jenna: The video I told you about went viral again. I guess a streamer reacted to a clip and the whole video got a bunch of views suddenly.

Eric: Are you okay?

Jenna: Yeah, thankfully someone, maybe Thomas, removed it from MyVid.

I clenched my fists. When I saw the video was going viral again on MyVid, I immediately reached out to a contact I had there to get it removed. At the time, I didn't know why it went viral—that Trekster reacted to a clip compilation. I just had to do something before people said anything else about her.

I was about to go live when I noticed it. Reading the comments, I was livid. I wanted to go to her and hold her, but all I could do was try to help. Then, when I messaged her about *Assassin's Creed,* I did so as EHucker. I never thought to do it as Eric.

Eric: I'm sorry, Jenna. What can I do?

Jenna: Nothing. I'm okay now. But I made a decision.

Eric: About what?

Jenna: I took what you said to heart. I am tired of hiding. The video being reposted upset me at first, but today when I woke up, I didn't have an overwhelming fear of what anyone would say. I just wanted to get ready to play in the next Button Mashers tournament. As myself.

Eric: I'm so proud of you, Jenna. I'll support you a hundred percent.

Jenna: Thank you. I also have this friend who isn't forthcoming with showing others his identity, and it seems to be really weighing on him. I thought if I could tell him about this, then maybe it would help him with whatever he is going through.

I read the text over and over. I wish I could tell her it wouldn't change anything.

A gust of wind blasted my face and snapped me out of my daydream. I couldn't feel my toes.

I marched inside and threw my phone on the bed. I ran my hand through my hair. If she knew I was the one that took the video down and that I was the one that was hiding away, she'd be furious I had lied, especially after everything she shared with me. I was being fake. I was encouraging her to be herself when I was doing the exact opposite.

My phone lit up. I walked over and picked it up.

Jenna: I have to get back to work. I'll talk to you soon. <3

My curser blinked, waiting for a reply. My heart squeezed.

Eric: Have a good day, beautiful.

I clicked the phone off, walked into my bathroom, and turned the shower on. The temperature didn't matter; I couldn't feel anything.

I removed my clothes and stepped into the stream of cool water. As I lathered up, my mind wouldn't stop racing with all the possibilities of what could happen if Jenna found out my secret. She wouldn't be able to get EHucker to come into the light, because I would quit before I reached the face cam goal. I just needed to make a little more to pay my parents back.

My chest tightened. I stepped out of the shower, dried off, and put on some shorts. I leaned on the vanity and stared at myself in the mirror, trying to regain my focus, but it was all too much. The darkness I was trying to avoid pushed through a corner of my mind. It did not ask for permission to enter, just shoved its way in, destroying everything in its path.

I gave in.

You're nothing now.

The person in the mirror looked like me, yet I didn't recognize his eyes. They were empty. The voice in my head proceeded to assault me.

You are not worthy of someone like Jenna. She is facing her past while you are running. Hiding. Avoiding your best friend. How can you encourage her when you have no intention of telling her who you really are? She'll leave you.

I grabbed the mirror off the wall and slammed it to the ground. It shattered around my bare feet. Breathing heavily, I gripped the edges of the sink.

Slowly the reality of what I did cleared the darkness and brought me back to myself and my surroundings.

My phone buzzed on the counter. I jolted. I grabbed my phone and read the Discord message.

Trekster: Yo, dude! You're late!

I blinked.

My phone buzzed again.

Trekster: Are you okay?

No. I wasn't. I was very much not okay. But there was no time to deal with it. I had forgotten about Trekster when the darkness took over. An enemy in my mind. I couldn't see anything else. I couldn't see at all.

EHucker360: Can you stall for five minutes?

Trekster: Five minutes. See you soon.

I gingerly stepped over the glass and rushed to put on shoes. I returned and picked up the biggest pieces of glass and swept up what I could. After streaming I would vacuum to make sure I hadn't missed any shards.

Exactly five minutes later, I joined Trekster's Discord channel.

"Sorry I'm late. Lost track of time."

"Bro, changing it up? Coming out?" Trekster asked, surprise in his voice.

"Coming out? What are you talking about?"

"Your voice. It's nice. A lot better than that voice changer. The ladies would swarm your stream with that tone. It's been years since I've heard it, back when you started, so I couldn't remember."

"Shoot!" I quickly flipped on the voice changer and glanced at my other monitor. I hadn't started my stream yet. I blew out a sigh of relief.

The panic I'd felt, thinking I almost revealed myself, well, that told me everything I needed to know. I couldn't share who I was with anyone. Maybe I could cancel the goal...

And the breakdown? Yeah, that was a lapse. I had everything under control now. I was fine.

"Sorry," I told Trekster.

"No need to apologize. I got you."

Trekster paused for a minute.

"I don't get it, E. What would happen if you decided to use the mic and cam. Are you a criminal or something?"

I snorted. That was the same thing Jenson thought.

"No. I just..."

Trekster didn't wait for me to continue.

"No worries. Let's get it."

We logged into the game, and I joined his lobby. We were going to play a couple of matches with our top subscribers.

"Trekster?" I said.

"Hmm?"

"That reaction video you posted. The one clip in it..."

"Oh. Yeah, that one clip is terrible."

I shook my head even though he couldn't see me.

"That's the woman I'm dating. Her ex made that video years ago."

"No kidding? I'll take the video down. No problem."

"I wasn't asking."

Trekster knew me better than that.

"Too late. It's gone."

"Just like that?"

"Yes, just like that. You're my best friend. No questions asked, except... you didn't tell me you asked her out."

"I haven't had the chance."

"I'm glad. Does she know who you are?"

My silence said everything.

"Then you might want to ask yourself is she worth it? If she doesn't know every version of you, then how can you be open to whatever this relationship may bring?

Trekster didn't know about my plans to quit, that in a couple of months, it wouldn't matter anymore.

"Let's just get started," I said.

"Okay, man. Oh! Before we open things up to our chat, I wanted to tell you something."

"Okay. What's going on?"

"I won't be online for the next two weeks. I'll be traveling with TakeNote, checking out players for this SimmerzCon competition. It's promotional, and a great way to meet some of these up-and-comers."

"Wow, that's great. Do you know where you're going?" What were the chances he'd end up at Button Mashers to check out Jenna?

"No. My assistant has it all covered. I know a few places we're heading to. Other than that, it'll be a quick cross-country tour."

"That's cool, man. It'll be fun to go with TakeNote."

I was a big supporter of TakeNote. She was one of the few streamers I connected with and played with from time to time. I would love to see TakeNote and Jenna play side by side. The other teams wouldn't stand a chance.

"Yeah. I've met her a couple of times at events and stuff. My girlfriend, Tara, is coming with us. She and TakeNote are like best friends. Taking a bus and everything, just the three of us and our assistants."

That sounded like a lot of fun. I knew SimmerzCon wanted

me to show up for them. It was known that Trekster and I were friends. I could have easily been preparing for the tour with him.

"Well, that's all. Let's start," he said.

We turned on our streams and welcomed our chat. It was a slightly smaller crowd for the morning. I saw on the viewer list that Jenson was watching. She must have been watching at the coffee shop between helping customers. My heart jumped into my throat.

Our moderators pulled in the first two players, and we began the game. We went at it for a couple of hours with a number of subscribers. Some of the players surprised me, doing as well as we did. Others we had to carry. All in all, we enjoyed giving back to our communities this way.

When we were done, we switched back to our private Discord call.

"I wish you could join us on tour," he said.

"Me too." I so wanted to be there for Trekster like he had been there for me all these years.

"Well, no worries," he said, back to his cheerful self. "Want to do this again next week?" he joked.

"Please, no."

Trekster laughed. "Later."

He disconnected from our call. I removed my headset and sat back in my chair.

My mind was whirling from the events of the morning. I was torn between doing what I should and sticking to my original plan to stream for a couple of years, pay off my medical bills, support my parents, then move on with my life.

The only problem was, I was stuck in a hamster wheel. Running but never moving forward. I only knew how to do what I had always done.

I got up and finished cleaning the bathroom. Exhausted from the emotional turmoil and the lack of sleep from the previous night, I collapsed on my bed. Then my phone buzzed.

Jenson: Great stream. I'm glad you stuck around.
She stayed. She stayed. She stayed...
I closed my eyes and fell asleep instantly.

Chapter Seventeen

JENNA

A couple of weeks had passed since I decided to enter the next Button Mashers tournament as myself, and finally, tonight was the night. I was able to spend time with Eric one day last week, and the other nights I practiced with EHucker. I even jumped in a random duos match and used my mic. I had a good game and a normal conversation with my male teammate. Despite all the preparation, I still worried that with the video going viral again, I would be recognized and discredited as a valid competitor. Especially if Carter had seen it.

When I arrived at Button Mashers, I sat at the bar to talk with Lewis. I dressed as myself in jeans, a zip jacket, and Converse. My hands had itched to grab a hat when I left, but Alyssa convinced me to leave it at home.

"I'm so nervous," I told Lewis.

"You? Nervous? That's not like you."

"I know! But it's different this time."

I eyed Carter, who'd already claimed his spot. While he wasn't allowed to sit down and get ready yet, he could still hover nearby. I turned away before he could notice me.

Lewis did a double take. "Wait, you're not..."

"Nope, I'm just Jenna tonight."

Lewis flashed a bright smile. "That's great. Is Eric coming?" Lewis set a glass of water down in front of me.

"Yeah. I asked him to show up right before the tournament started. I needed time to mentally prepare." I took a sip.

"You'll do great. These guys won't know what hit them."

The door opened, and I expected to see Eric. Instead, a woman who looked to be my age walked in, wearing a sleek designer pantsuit. Despite looking out of place, she did a quick survey of the room then marched to the bar with an air of confidence.

"I'll have a blueberry Moscow mule, please, with fresh mint," she said to Lewis.

Lewis gave me a sideways glance and cleared his throat. "We don't have that. I could offer you a beer or a rum and Coke if you're looking for something with liquor."

She bit her bottom lip. Lewis's gaze dropped to her mouth. Interesting.

"I guess I'll take the rum and Coke." She slid onto the barstool next to me.

"Good choice. I'm Jenna."

"Ella." Her eyes flared in recognition. "You work at Three Beans Coffee Shop."

I immediately recalled her and her full order. "That's right. Did you make it to wherever you were going?"

She laughed. "Barely, but I did." She turned her attention back to Lewis, who had knocked over a glass. He muttered something before grabbing a highball glass to make her drink. "What's up with him?"

"Lewis? Not sure."

I tried to hide my amusement. Every chance he got, he looked over at Ella.

"I didn't mean to upset him. I thought this was a full bar."

"Well, Lewis owns the place. It's still growing, but the main offering is the in-house beers."

"He owns it? That's so awesome." She took another look around the bar.

"First time here?"

"Is it that obvious? Yeah. It was on my way home. Bad day. Thought maybe I needed some fun in my life."

"This is a good place to find it. I'm actually about to game in the monthly tournament."

"Oh really? Go you!"

"Yeah, gonna show these guys what's up." I gave her a brilliant smile.

Ella laughed right as Lewis returned with her drink. His eyes shifted from me to her as he tried to figure out the joke.

Ella took a sip, her eyes going wide. "Wow, this is so good. Thanks."

"You're welcome."

"I'm Ella." She stuck out her hand.

"Lewis," he grunted out.

It was like I'd disappeared from existence.

Ella turned back to me and stood up from her seat. "I'm gonna go check out the arcade. Nice to meet you, Jenna." She made her way over there without a second glance to Lewis.

Lewis smacked himself in the forehead. "Stupid, stupid, stupid."

"You weren't that bad."

"She thinks I'm an idiot."

"No, she actually thought it was awesome that you own the brewery. I thought you were good at this flirting thing," I teased.

"But she's..." All he could do after that was sputter.

"Hey Jenna," said Eric, coming up to the bar. I stood up and faced him. He pulled me into a hug. "Are you ready?"

"Not sure. Though now that you're here, I feel ready." I kissed his cheek.

Eric leaned back and met my eyes. The same sadness I'd noticed before was still present.

"Are you okay?"

"What? Of course." The corner of his mouth tilted up, giving me the half smile I'd grown so familiar with. "Get in there and play your game. You got this. I'll be right here afterward."

I nodded and gave him one last hug. I turned toward the

consoles, but Eric stopped me and pulled me back into his arms. He held my face in his hands, leaned down, and kissed me long and hard. For a moment, I forgot everything. The bar melted away, and all I felt was Eric.

When he finally let me go, I took my place at my usual station. I synced my controller and plugged in my headset. (Controllers were provided, but most players preferred to use their own.) I glanced over my shoulder to find Eric watching me. The rest of the competitors were immersed in their setups. They hadn't seemed to notice their typical male competitor was not sitting in the corner this time or that some woman had taken his seat.

I logged in and gave myself a pep talk. *Play your game. Pay no mind to the others surrounding you. This is your chance to get to SimmerzCon.* The convention was inching closer, and they would decide soon enough who would make it.

I relaxed and waited for the first game to start. Tonight we would play as many games as we could in two hours. We received points in the tournament by placing in the top three, or one point for each elimination. All tournament points were connected to my Jenson gamertag, so it didn't matter that I was now sitting here as Jenna. This wasn't the type of match where you could hide until the end; you had to actively participate. I snorted at the irony.

I wondered if or when anyone would notice me. Maybe I would get in and out and it would not be a big deal. But then I thought about EHucker. Next time we talked, I would tell him about my newly found courage. I would tell him that I no longer cared about the video and that it didn't stop me from reaching my goals. Maybe then he would tell me what had caused him to go as far as using a voice changer as well as no camera.

I turned around and looked for Eric. He stood at the bar, chatting with Lewis, but his eyes were on me. He nodded encouragingly, but I was worried about him. He was here physically but it seemed that his head was elsewhere tonight.

I faced my screen and queued in for the game. Time to focus.

I started off playing skillfully, but I wasn't hitting my stride. I won two games and lost one. Each time I had a decent number of kills, which put me at the top of the leaderboard with Carter. I struggled in the second half but managed to pull off another win with high kill streaks in each match.

When all the matches were complete, I waited for the final scores to be tallied then loaded onto the screen near the bar. The winner was...

"Nah, nah, nah! Again?" Carter squeaked.

This was what I worried about, but I wouldn't hide. Not this time.

"No way, Jenson! Show yourself! I want to know who you are."

Carter stood behind his chair, analyzing each of the competitors within his field of view. He didn't see me in the corner. No one did, as everyone was staring at Carter.

Ready to face the inevitable, I pulled off my headset and stood from my seat. "Me. I'm Jenson," I called out.

Carter scanned the room again but couldn't figure out who had spoken. "Who?"

"I said I'm Jenson!" I stepped forward from my seat, making it very clear. He pinned his eyes on me.

"You? Are you kidding me? *You're* Jenson?" He marched over and stood in front of me. Too close. I shuddered at the way he scanned my body. He looked half angry and half lecherous.

Trembling slightly, I stood my ground.

I released a breath when I felt a warm presence at my side. Then I inhaled a whiff of pine and sandalwood, a scent I had become so comfortable with.

"You'll want to think carefully about what you say next to my girlfriend."

My eyes darted to Eric. He hadn't officially asked me to be his girlfriend, but I wasn't upset at the declaration. It was the natural progression of our dating. I glanced past Carter to Lewis, who watched from the bar. He threw his towel down his eyes blazing.

Carter ignored Eric. "Didn't a dude used to game in this spot?"

"It's been me, not a dude."

Carter's eyebrows shot up. "You're the one who's been beating me?"

I nodded.

Carter scoffed. "Unbelievable."

Eric stepped closer. "What's that supposed to mean?"

Carter sized up Eric. "It's just unbelievable *she* has been the one winning all these tournaments. And who are you exactly?"

"I'm Eric Slayter."

Carter turned back to me and snapped his fingers. "I thought you looked familiar. You're that girl from that video. Your hair is different, but you're her. You're Trained Girl!"

The other competitors all looked at me and started whispering to each other. I looked down, trying to hide myself again. Then a voice I recognized but never expected sliced through the tension.

"Ah, who cares about that old video some idiot made?" said Trekster, and I whipped my head up. "This woman is amazing, and she's tonight's champion!"

The crowd that had gathered around us parted and there stood Trekster beside TakeNote with a huge grin on his face.

Trekster and TakeNote were at Button Mashers!

Chapter Eighteen

ERIC

I was taken aback at the sight of Trekster and TakeNote.

"If you're done, we have something to discuss with Jenson," Trekster said to Carter with narrowed eyes.

"You'll pay for this," Carter said, glaring at me, then sauntered to the bar.

I didn't know what he meant, but as long as it wasn't directed at Jenna, I didn't care.

Trekster was now staring at me, grinning from ear to ear.

When Trekster told me he was looking for SimmerzCon competitors, I didn't think of what could happen if he showed up here. He was sharp. Apparently he remembered I was seeing the woman from that video he watched, and when Carter called her out, that was confirmation.

"Hey, Jenson. I'm Trekster." He offered his hand and she shook it, followed by TakeNote, who also introduced herself.

"Yes, I... I know who you are. I'm Jenna. I've been watching your stream for years, TakeNote."

"I recognized your name from my stream. I recall you chatting from time to time."

Jenna's eyes lit up.

"I'm Eric," I jumped in.

"Sorry, this is Eric, my boyfriend. But what are you guys doing here?"

"Right," Trekster said. "We're checking out potential competitors for SimmerzCon. Talking to them about it."

"That's awesome. I'm glad you're here," said Jenna.

"How have you been preparing for the tournament?" Take-Note asked.

"Participating in Button Masher tournaments of course. And at home, I've been playing with someone you're well-acquainted with, Trekster: EHucker."

My stomach dropped. This was it.

"Oh yeah. He's my guy! A really great dude."

"Have you met him?" Jenna asked.

"Nope. He's super private. Even to me. Love the guy though. Wait, you play games with him regularly?"

"Yeah. Why? Is that a problem for the tournament?"

Trekster's eyes met mine for a brief moment, and I panicked.

"No. No problem at all. Anyway, TakeNote, do you want to tell her more about SimmerzCon?"

"Yes of course." As TakeNote started giving Jenna more details about the event, Trekster pointed toward the arcade.

"Yo, Eric. Want to race?"

"I'll be back," I told Jenna, kissing her on the head.

She grinned and returned her attention to TakeNote.

In the arcade, we sat in the tall seats of the racing game, shielding us from the rest of the bar.

"Is it really you, bro?" The excitement in his voice was undeniable.

"Yeah, it is."

"Dude!"

"Keep it down, would you? I still haven't told her."

"Why not? You know what? Doesn't matter. I'm so happy to meet you." He hugged me awkwardly, sitting side by side. But it was long overdue.

"Same, man." I patted him on the back.

"Jenna is fantastic. She has a real shot at SimmerzCon. But what's with that guy? He's a real piece of work."

"Carter was lucky—if you hadn't shown up when you did, I might have decked him."

Trekster eyed me for a second before turning forward. "You know, you're not what I expected."

I laughed. "What were you expecting?"

"I don't know. I know you said it wasn't your looks, but I expected something that stood out. Like maybe you were insecure about being scrawny or you had a peg leg or something. But dude. You're freaking hot."

I burst out laughing. Only Trekster could get away with compliments like that without it being embarrassing. "I'm still figuring things out. I'm really happy to finally meet you too."

"I didn't think this day would ever come. And now that it has, I am solidifying our forever friendship." He pounded fists with me.

Despite the surprise of him showing up, I was glad to meet Trekster. He was as genuine in person as he was online.

"Now that we got that out of the way, let's race!" he said, pointing at the game before us.

We began and chose our cars. After a couple of races, we talked about life and the tour. Tara had to work but would be joining him for the back half on the road.

I was about to suggest we get back to Jenna and TakeNote when I heard a joyful voice behind me.

"Enjoying the game?" Jenna asked.

I gulped: She'd removed her jacket to reveal a black silk blouse, and she had applied the same red lipstick from our date.

On my other side, Trekster hit my arm. "Quit drooling and let's get drinks." He hopped up from his seat.

When I got up to follow him, Jenna stopped me. "You guys hit it off quickly."

"Yeah. He's an easy guy to get along with."

She stepped forward and placed her hands on my chest.

I wrapped my arms around her. "Thank you for being here tonight." She touched her cheek to my chest, and I rested my chin atop her head.

Letting go, she bounced on her toes. "Guess what!"

"What?"

"TakeNote told me they allow everyone to bring a guest to SimmerzCon. Would you want to go if I get in?" She stared at me, hope and excitement coming off her like heat.

I couldn't go. People would know who I was. If they saw EHucker there... No. She wants me, Eric, to go with her, not EHucker. I spent so much time talking to her as EHucker when I thought about her in the gaming space, I thought of myself as EHucker instead of myself. This was getting confusing.

"Yeah, I could probably go," I said slowly.

"Great!" She lifted herself up on her tiptoes and gave me a quick kiss. "I'm ready to get out of here but not ready for the night to end. Do you want to come over?" There was no way I could refuse with that glint in her eye.

"I'd love that." I grabbed her hand and led her to the bar to get her things.

We told TakeNote and Trekster goodbye. Knowing he couldn't say much, Trekster shook my hand and winked at me. Jenna asked me what that was about. I told her he was a funny guy and liked joking around.

We waved to Lewis, but he didn't see us, as he was staring at a woman watch a group of teens play *Mario Kart*.

"Who's that?" I asked.

"Ella. She's new here. She came in tonight after work for a cocktail. Lewis might be a goner."

I glanced at Jenna. I could understand the sentiment. Goner was right.

Chapter Nineteen

JENNA

Back at my house, I fumbled with the keys, trying to unlock the door. I felt like my whole body was still shaking from tonight's events. Even though Carter was confrontational, as expected, and mentioned the video, Eric stepped up, and Trekster shut down further conversation quickly.

When I spoke with TakeNote about SimmerzCon, I realized something: I no longer cared if Thomas would be there or not. I loved gaming. I had since I was little and Matt put the N64 controller in my hand. I wanted to compete and do well, if only to prove to myself that I didn't have to hide. I could be myself and be okay with whatever anyone said about me. It didn't matter anymore.

TakeNote filled me in on some of the details, that if I made it, I would be paired with two other streamers for the competition. The schedule of events sounded like a gamer's dream. I wanted to do everything in my power to qualify, and winning tonight put me one step closer.

I invited Eric back to my house to hang out, but I was still worried something was going on with him. I hoped that I could get him to open up.

I finally got my door unlocked and pushed it open. "Welcome to my little house," I said, ushering him inside.

I'd rented a cute little two-bedroom, the perfect amount of space for me. With Eric here, the house felt smaller, as his athletic build had quite the presence. When he'd picked me up for our date, he only stepped into the foyer.

"Do you want any tea?" I gestured toward the living room couch.

"Sure," he replied with a small smile.

"What kind? Green? Chamomile? Lemon and honey?"

"Green is good."

I busied myself with heating the water and adding the tea. It steeped for a couple of minutes, then I brought the two mugs to the living room and set them on the coffee table.

Eric grabbed his and took a sip. "I don't drink a lot of tea, but I always love a hot drink."

"I love tea at night. It's calming, and this kind doesn't have caffeine."

We sat in comfortable silence for a minute.

Eric pointed to the picture on my side table. "Your brother?"

I nodded. Matt was twelve years old in the photo. (I was eight at the time.) His head was tilted back, laughing at something someone had said. He was always joyful. It was so infectious.

"If Matt were still alive, do you think he'd be a pro gamer? He got you into gaming. Would you be doing what you're doing now?"

I paused. Right after Matt's death, I had wondered what my life would look like. Maybe I wouldn't be gaming as much. Maybe I would have taken a slightly different path. It seemed nonsensical to think in those terms.

"Matt would have probably been an entrepreneur like Lewis. Or inventing something to help people. He couldn't stay still for long. He was a dreamer and cared about everyone. I like to imagine he would be doing something good in the world."

Eric nodded.

"Sometimes I still struggle with the what-ifs about Matt. But ultimately, I can't let them stop me from doing what I want to do. Maybe it would be different if he were here, but dwelling on that is not going to change anything. Maybe I was always meant to love gaming."

I shrugged and took a sip of my tea. "My point is, if we keep looking to the past to try to figure out who we think we should be, we'll miss out on who we're supposed to be now and the excitement of moving forward."

Eric shook his head. "But you let your past with Thomas change how you live now. At least, until tonight."

I set down my tea and glanced over at my Xbox setup. I thought about the past weeks and how much my desires had changed. I thought the video always labeled me and what I was capable of but instead it just left me bitter. With the encouragement of Eric and opening myself to play games with EHucker, I was able to be myself tonight.

"You're right. I did hide. I let that video haunt me, and it influenced how I felt about everyone around me. I thought I needed to get back at Thomas, but really, I needed to just let go. I didn't know it at the time, but the first moment we met you knew who I was, and being Jenson never mattered to you."

"You're right, it didn't."

"Why?"

Eric stood up, blew out a breath, and paced up and down my living room. "I guess I understood you. And at the same time, I didn't. I wanted to know why someone as bright as you snuffed out her own light."

I furrowed my brows. "You understood me?"

Eric didn't answer my question. He ran his hand through his hair again, and his breathing grew heavier. I set down my tea.

"Eric, what's wrong?"

He halted and faced me. "You are so amazing, you know that? I'm not even half the person you are."

"Eric, you're wonderful. What are you talking about?"

He resumed pacing. Then he stopped, his back to me.

"I can't do this anymore," he choked out.

"Do what? Eric, you're scaring me."

He sat back down on the couch with his face in his hands, taking long breaths in and out. I wrapped my arms around him.

"Tell me what's going on. Please."

He sat up and stared forward. "I've been dreaming about my accident again."

"Why didn't you tell me?" I reached out and grabbed his hand.

"Because I didn't want you to know." He hesitated and shook his head. "I'm angry I'll never snowboard again, and that my career is truly over. The vision I had for my life is gone. Here you are, talking about moving forward after you lost someone special, your brother. And here I am, complaining about missing something that's a hobby for most people."

"It doesn't matter that our pain is different. It's still important."

"But I don't know how to move forward."

I squeezed his hand, eager to help. "What do you want to do? What else do you like? You said you do freelance video editing. Maybe you can turn that into your new passion."

Eric stood and walked over to my window, his back to me. I stood up too.

"I... lied," he whispered.

"What?"

"I lied," he said more clearly. "I don't freelance. I do video editing but just on my own content." He faced me now, looking directly at me. "I'm a gamer, Jenna. But not only a gamer—I'm also a streamer."

I took a step back in shock. "You're... what? You stream?"

"Yes."

"You have a small following?"

"No. My stream has really taken off.

"You're popular? I would have thought I'd know."

"You do."

I took a deep breath. My mind raced with the possibilities. But I've only ever mentioned a few streamers to him and Trekster and TakeNote were back at Button Mashers. Then it hit me. No. He couldn't be. "You're EHucker?"

I waited. Waited for him to deny it. Waited for him to tell me he was someone else I hadn't heard of. He slumped his shoulders and jammed his hands into his pockets, his eyes downcast. The sadness and regret in his expression gutted me. I didn't know what to make of it.

"I am."

I took another step back and turned away, giving myself time to think.

Eric was EHucker. EHucker was Eric. I tried to jog my memory, to remember all the things I'd told EHucker. Why hadn't Eric ever said anything? Shoot. One of the first things I said was I avoided guys who gamed. I liked Eric. I think I would have understood. But maybe not. I had blinders on at the brewery to avoid any romantic entanglements—until Eric. EHucker was very private about himself to the point of using a voice changer. I planned to tell EHucker about hiding myself, to get him to open up, but he knew about all that because he was... Eric. Why?

I spun around to ask him, but he was already gone.

Chapter Twenty

ERIC

I rolled over in bed, the buzzing of my phone waking me from a nightmare. It was Justin calling yet again. For once I hesitated with my thumb hovering over the answer button. After all this time, he still hadn't given up even though I was a terrible friend. Instead of answering, I hit *Ignore* and silenced my phone.

After I admitted to Jenna that I was EHucker, I bolted. Her gaping mouth and her silence said it all. I couldn't stick around to hear her say it. We were done. I'd lied to her. All because I wanted a chance. More than that, though, I didn't want to face the reality that was becoming so abundantly clear since she walked into my life.

I couldn't conceal my identity forever.

She was the beacon that pierced through all my darkness. And the closer I got to her, the more this gloom bled into my life, making it impossible to ignore. I finally started to feel alive again, and it was so utterly painful.

Except with her, I was happy. It was enough to outweigh the pain. But now I was back to square one, unable to numb myself with the cold.

I groaned. It was two in the afternoon. After I got home in the evening, I did something unheard of: I drank. A lot. Last night was too much to bear, so I used alcohol to soften the blow and passed out.

There was a sharp pounding sound in my head that continued in small spurts. After a moment, I realized it wasn't my head but my front door.

I dragged myself out of bed, intent on telling off this intruder, but when I swung the door open, I couldn't move, much less speak. Jenna stood there looking as stunning as ever, in dark jeans that hugged her curves and a fuzzy maroon sweater I wanted to reach out and touch.

She gazed at me, caution in her eyes. I blinked, overwhelmed by her beauty. But then I snapped out of it and became acutely aware of my disheveled appearance. I reeked of alcohol and had the worst case of bedhead.

"Can I come in?"

"Sure." I stepped back and cringed. Empty beer bottles lined the counter, and a partial bottle of tequila was resting against the arm of the couch. Oh, yeah. That was when things had taken a turn for the worse.

She picked up the bottle and set it on my kitchen counter. I swallowed. "I wasn't expecting to see you. Do you mind—uh—I need ten minutes."

"No problem."

I booked it out of the room and closed my bedroom door. I stripped off my clothes then took the fastest shower of my life, all the while trying to collect my thoughts.

What was she doing here? Did she want to make it clear we were over? Did she come to yell at me?

I could feel the darkness closing in on me, so I distracted myself by moving faster. I shoved my legs into some jersey shorts and pulled on a clean T-shirt. I brushed my teeth, staring at my mirrorless wall, and dashed back out to the living room.

She was gone. And my kitchen was clean. All the beer bottles had been recycled, and the dishwasher was running.

I ran my hand through my wet hair, frustrated with myself. Why did I think it mattered if I was clean or not when the love of my life had walked through my door?

Wait. Love of my life? The realization hit me so swiftly I audibly gasped. But yes. She was.

I turned to lock myself back in my room, when I noticed the door to my streaming room was open. I peered inside. She was standing there staring at all my equipment. The two monitors, the camera I had bought and never used, my microphone. My controllers sat on their chargers for when I felt like playing a game with a controller instead of a mouse and keyboard. The whole setup.

I cleared my throat.

She whipped her head around.

"Sorry about that. You didn't have to clean up for me. I'm embarrassed."

"Don't be." She shrugged and turned back to look around the room. "This is amazing, you know. You had the setup the whole time to stream with a camera, as yourself."

I crossed my arms over my chest and nodded.

"Why don't you? Why wait until you reach your face cam goal?"

"Can we go sit in the living room?"

"Sure."

"Would you like a drink, some coffee maybe?"

"No thanks," she said as she plopped down on the couch. In the kitchen, I grabbed my strongest roast and dumped heaping scoops of grounds into the machine, then joined her while it brewed.

"Look Jenna, I'm sorry I didn't tell you."

"Why did you leave last night without saying anything?"

"I figured you didn't want to see me anymore."

She paused. "I'm sorry. I was clear about not wanting to date guys who played video games—that had to factor in to why you kept things under wraps. But I don't feel that way anymore. I like you, Eric. And my friendship with EHucker was just as important. Now that I know you're the same person, it all fits.

You've seen both sides of me. Fully. So now I only want to know why. Why are you hiding?"

I grimaced. "You not wanting to date gamers wasn't the only reason. It's not even a main reason."

I stared down at my feet, trying to come up with what to say that would make sense to her. She placed her hand on my knee, which, I didn't realize until that moment, was bouncing restlessly.

"Tell me everything. I want to understand." She slowly stroked her thumb across my knee and waited patiently as I gathered my thoughts.

I would either need to confess or lose her. Her coming here gave me a glimmer of hope. I placed my hand on hers and started from the beginning.

"I've told you about snowboarding and my accident. What I didn't tell you was what came after. I was devastated. First there was my recovery, which was a haze—I was on a lot of pain meds, so I don't remember most of it. When I was finally well enough to start moving around, I began physical therapy. I got up every day, motivated to heal and get back on my board. I thought things were going well until I went to a follow-up appointment with my doctor."

I blew out a breath. Jenna flipped her palm around and grasped my hand.

"The injuries to my knee were extensive. My doctor told me I would never be able to return to snowboarding. After that, my life blew up. ESPN and other media swarmed my family, asking too many questions. Every day it was a reminder of the dream I could no longer have."

"Why would they do that?"

"I was a new pro in the sport, one of the hottest snowboarders to watch. In that world, it was big news. But my sponsorships dried up, the core group of guys I hung out with got bored, and my girlfriend dumped me." She wrinkled her nose. "Don't worry, losing the girlfriend was the least of it."

"So what brought on streaming and disguising yourself?"

"Well, that was sort of a happy accident. I had been Trekster's moderator for a long time, and I told him, in not so many words, what happened. He encouraged me to stream to make a few bucks during my recovery, but then my followers really started growing. When I set goals, my viewers seemed to like it. I made the face cam goal in the beginning, not ever intending to reach it. I planned to be done streaming by then."

"But you're so close. You can't quit now. So many people want to know who you are."

"I *know*." I sighed. "I know."

"I don't get it. What will happen if you show your face? And why didn't you tell me? Why pursue getting to know me online?"

The coffee machine beeped so I got up to pour myself a cup of black coffee. I offered some to her again, and this time she nodded. I knew she wouldn't turn down coffee. I couldn't help but smile a little. I added the cream and sugar I knew she liked and returned to the living room with our mugs.

She took hers and sipped it slowly. I watched her as I drank. The bitterness seemed to slow the pounding in my head.

"The reason I streamed anonymously was partly because I didn't want reporters to find me. I didn't want to draw any attention to myself. Moving away helped. The second reason..." I rubbed my forehead. "I didn't want to face myself. If I didn't show anyone who I was, I could get by. I wasn't fake, but I had to pull from somewhere deep to be present. Some days are better than others. Some days I forget what I once wanted. Other days it still hurts like it happened yesterday."

I rubbed my knee. Jenna placed her hand over mine, calming me into stopping.

"When I met you, that changed everything," I said. "I saw part of myself in you, and I couldn't ignore it. When we talked, I thought I would find someone similar to myself. Instead, I found the opposite. That's why I spoke to you as EHucker. When I saw you in my stream, I couldn't ignore you. I asked you to play a game with me before thinking it through."

Her eyes searched mine. What she was hoping to find I didn't know.

I continued: "It wasn't that I was withholding information from just you, it was from everyone. But as time went on, and as I encouraged you to be yourself, I realized that I could no longer ignore the mask that I had on in front of others. It was killing me."

"That's why you asked me to stay," Jenna said, looking concerned.

"Yes, I was contemplating stopping streaming for good. But I didn't want to lose you. Not just you, Jenna, but the connection we had through gaming."

"So now are you going to stop streaming?"

I got up and looked out the window, noticing the snow had melted. There was nothing I could numb myself with.

"No. I still have more that I owe," I said.

"Owe?"

"To my family. I have to make everything right."

"Eric, I don't think—"

"It's fine, Jenna." I turned back to her. "I'll still quit before I hit my face cam goal, and then we can leave this all in the past."

Hurt flashed across her face.

"I didn't mean us." I sat back down next to her and took her hand in mine. "I want to be with you. If all this didn't scare you off. If you can forgive me, will you stay with me?"

She let out a sigh. "Eric, of course. I care about you. I understand. It makes sense that we have a natural connection. But I want to get to know you better, all of you. Don't ever lie to me again. Please."

"I will always be honest with you, one hundred percent. But

I still can't reveal myself to anyone else. Not yet. Please don't tell anyone."

Jenna stared at me, and I started to sweat.

"Okay, I won't tell. When you're ready, I'll be there like you were for me."

I pulled Jenna into a hug. "Thank you."

I kissed her head, but then she pulled back and pressed her lips to mine. I kissed her back, relieved. She forgave me. She was still here.

When we broke apart, she blushed. "Eric..."

"Let me take you out. No more lies. You get all of me," I said.

She nodded, then curled up and leaned on my shoulder. I wrapped my arms around her and relaxed. I held on to her for as long as I could.

Chapter Twenty-One

JENNA

Ever since Eric revealed to me that he was EHucker, things had been great between us. We still played video games together, and we still went out on dates. Except now I didn't have to be anyone else with him, and neither did he.

Then Friday night happened.

I was sitting on my couch, watching his stream on my phone. I always learned new ways to move across the map that I couldn't see before. I perked up when someone dropped his community into Eric's stream.

"AndrewKy with a drop-in. Welcome! My name is EHucker, and I mainly stream *Total Command*."

The new viewers typed their greetings into the chat, and several gifted subs. The numbers in his face cam goal climbed.

"Thank you," Eric said. "You don't have to do that. But thank you for the subs."

The new viewers calmed down, and Eric started another match. He captured his first objective just as another community dropped in.

"I see PaigesInTime is dropping in with a hundred and fifty viewers."

Eric introduced himself again, and more subs were gifted.

I set down my phone and leaned forward.

It was then that I knew something extraordinary was happening, because in the next twenty minutes, Eric had six more communities drop in, each with over one hundred viewers. None of them were bots either. With each drop-in, subs were gifted until the number ticked past his goal.

"No way," I said out loud.

The chat was chaos, with everyone typing *"Face Cam! Face Cam! Face Cam!"*

I grabbed my phone and almost fumbled it to the floor. I opened my texts, but I wasn't sure what to say to Eric. Should I encourage him? Let him know I was here for him? What was he going to do?

He had been adamant about quitting before reaching this milestone, but part of me thought he should do it. I hadn't realized how much my past was weighing me down until I set my fears aside and entered the Button Masher's tournament as myself, regardless of what people thought of the video. Maybe if Eric revealed himself, he would finally unburden himself.

Before I could type anything, he spoke through the voice changer.

"Thanks for a great stream, everyone. I'll catch you next time."

Still in the middle of a match, he ended his stream. He didn't even use his catchphrase.

Jenna: Are you okay?

Minutes passed with no response. I got up and started pacing, while checking my phone every few seconds.

Eric: Yup. Why wouldn't I be?

Jenna: What are you going to do about meeting your face cam goal?

Several more minutes passed, and I started to wonder if I should drive over there.

Eric: I'm really tired from streaming. I'm gonna catch some Z's. Good night, Jenna.

Tears were welling up. He was shutting me out. I put down my phone and got ready for bed.

The pressure had been rising for him as the goal inched closer;

he became more closed off and quiet whenever I brought up his stream. I didn't understand why he didn't quit, but he insisted he hadn't fixed things yet. He claimed he owed his family, but I wondered if they felt that way. I didn't get that kind of impression from Emily, at least.

Eric was digging himself into a hole. At what point would he say it was enough?

A month later

Eric's robotic voice rang through the screen: "See ya! Keep grinding."

The face cam goal was gone from his screen and replaced with a new goal. If he got 500 new subscribers on MyVid, he would do a giveaway for *Total Command* game currency.

Eric wouldn't talk to me about meeting the face cam goal—he always changed the subject. Even though he had removed it, his chat reminded him daily. Often he left his stream on subscribers-only mode, where only subs could type, but even then, he was questioned about it.

Responding to his chat, he'd come up with excuses, like not having the proper equipment or joking that no one really wanted to see his ugly mug. That didn't deter them much. Finally, he ignored it and started banning the harassers.

He lost a lot of regular viewers. And half of those still there were probably just curious if he would change his mind and hold true to his promise. He got called a liar and a scammer for not following through. It really compromised his reputation with the community he built.

Eric ended his stream, and I set my phone down and sighed.

I didn't push him to share his identity on camera, because I didn't think that was the main issue. He hadn't created a new dream from streaming, but a distraction. He was still holding on to the past.

My feelings for Eric had intensified, and I worried about him more. We could game, go out, laugh and have fun, but when it was time for him to stream, I saw the spark leave his eyes, and it killed me to see him like that.

I grabbed my purse and keys and headed out to Button Mashers to meet him, along with Alyssa and Bryan, who had picked a venue for their wedding, and we were going to discuss their plans.

When I arrived at the bar, Bryan and Alyssa were already there, chatting with Lewis, who slid me a drink as I approached.

"That's so exciting you set a date," I told Alyssa.

"I know, right? It's so far away, but it was the best they had for that venue."

"It'll be here before you know it, and there's a lot to do to get ready."

"I know! You know I can't do it alone. Which reminds me..." She rustled around her purse until she pulled out a small jewelry box.

"What's this?" I said, eying the box.

"Open it!" she practically squealed.

I lifted the lid. Inside was a beautiful white-gold heart necklace with an amethyst glistening in the center. A note on the underside of the lid read, *Will you be my maid of honor?*

"Of course!" We slid off our stools and hugged while jumping up and down. We got some looks from some people around the bar, but I didn't care. Bryan sipped his drink, unaffected by all the commotion.

Someone cleared their throat.

"What did I miss?" Eric joined our group, eyebrows raised.

Before I could say anything, Alyssa threw her arms around him and yelled, "She said yes!"

"What?"

"Jenna is going to be my maid of honor."

Eric chuckled. "Oh."

Bryan waved him over. "Come on, man. This is going to go on for months, and we're just getting started." Bryan pretended he was exasperated by the whole thing, but he was smiling.

Eric kissed me on the forehead then joined Bryan at the bar. He ordered a beer, and the three men talked among themselves.

Alyssa and I moved into the arcade, where we played games, sipped our drinks, and spoke about her wedding.

After a bit, Alyssa nudged me. "So has everyone been receptive since you competed in the last Button Mashers tournament?"

I looked around. A few guys from the tournament were here, immersed in their games.

"I haven't had any problems."

"Whatever happened with that online guy?"

My stomach jumped. I hadn't mentioned EHucker since the night he told me, and she hadn't brought him up until now, so I thought maybe she had forgotten about him. "We don't message anymore. I've been busy and haven't had time to game with him either." Part of that was true: I texted Eric directly; we didn't message on Discord anymore.

"Well, that doesn't matter. I have all the confidence in the world that you will make it into SimmerzCon."

"Thanks, Alyssa."

"So... how's it going with Eric?"

"I'm really happy." I looked over at him standing at the bar, and I couldn't help but smile.

"I'm glad. He seems like a great guy. Do you see it going the distance?"

"Yes. Maybe."

"Oh my gosh, you're in love!"

My face was instantly warm. "Shhh. Maybe," I said shyly.

We hadn't said that word, but the truth was I did love him. I just didn't want to be the first to say it.

"Jenna?"

I turned around to see a guy with light brown hair and a graphic tee peering down at me with bright hazel eyes.

"I'm Henry." He pulled a hand out of his jeans pockets, to shake mine. "I saw you at the Button Masher tournament last month and wanted to talk to you."

"Nice to meet you," I said warily. I still wasn't used to guys knowing I was Jenson. I never knew whether they were going to be judgmental like Carter, or friendly, or try to hit on me.

"I don't know if you recognize me at all, but I've played in tournaments here. I'm impressed by your gameplay. I can't believe I never noticed you're a woman."

I gave him a crooked shrug. "I meant for it to be that way."

He shuffled his feet. "I don't mean that as an insult. You're talented regardless. I was wondering if you'd want to pick up a couple of games online with me and my friends?"

"Sure."

"Great, I'll add you. My screen name is Lockout, so you know it's me. See you around." He walked back to the bar to rejoin his friends.

"What was that about?" said Eric, as he and Bryan came over.

Bryan wrapped an arm around Alyssa. She nuzzled his neck, and they walked away to play a round of *Ms. Pacman*.

"He wanted to add me as a friend online so we could play some matches."

Eric pinched his lips into a line. "Should I be worried?"

"Are you jealous?" I asked, arching an eyebrow.

He leaned down and kissed me. I melted against his strong chest and forgot about the activity around us.

When he finally pulled back a little, he was smiling. "I don't know. I remember you ended up falling for the last person you met online."

"Yes, because he was also an amazing guy I knew in person."

Stepping back, I nudged him. "You could always join our game, you know."

His smile faded. "You know I can't."

Since the face cam incident, Eric refused to play with others online, except for me. He ran solo matches whenever he was on stream. He wasn't even playing with Trekster. Eric had been invited to SimmerzCon as a streamer. If I got in, I wanted him to come and possibly be my partner in the competition, but his anonymity kept him from having the freedom to do any of that.

"Eric, maybe if we played with Henry it would be okay, and you could think about coming to SimmerzCon with me?"

"Jenna, no," he snapped.

I flinched at his tone. He looked around the arcade and ran his hand through his hair. I was losing him.

"I'm going to go."

"Eric, please."

"Sorry. I'm tired from streaming." His excuse as always. He gave me a chaste kiss and marched out the door, leaving me standing there.

Alyssa and Bryan walked up.

"What happened?" she asked.

"Everything okay?"

I collected myself and gave them a half smile. "Yeah, he has to get up early for work." I hated lying to my friends. And I hated that I couldn't tell them who he was and what happened with EHucker.

Alyssa chatted with me about the other women she planned on asking to be in the wedding party. I nodded along with her. When I stole a glance at Bryan, he looked at me knowingly. I didn't know what he knew, but it seemed he suspected something was up.

I returned my attention to Alyssa, but I couldn't concentrate. My heart ached for Eric. I wanted him to move forward from the past that plagued him. I could empathize, after all, and I wanted to help him as he helped me. I just didn't know how.

Chapter Twenty-Two

ERIC

I stood at the top of the tower, surveying the landscape. Spotting two players running through the middle of downtown, I took aim and eliminated each one with two quick sniper shots. I jumped off the building and deployed my parachute to get into the closing circle in time. I then ran into another building and began looting, and searching for more cash to buy a self-revive in the event someone knocked me down. Unlikely. But I could never be too careful. I was skilled in this game, not immune.

I opened a loot crate and grabbed another wad of money out of it. There was enough for the revive. I had just located a buy station on my map when my phone started buzzing on my desk.

I turned and looked at the screen: Justin. He hadn't called me in a couple of weeks. Part of me almost wondered what happened to him.

Almost.

I rejected the call.

I sprinted out the door and jumped into a vehicle to get to the next buy station.

I glanced at my chat. They were either cheering me on or saying obnoxious things about the game. Pretty typical.

I reached the buy station and bought the self-revive.

My phone buzzed again. I hit *End* to drop the call.

I ran inside another building and peeked out a window, searching for the other players. Gunfire in the distance. I dashed upstairs to get a better angle on my adversaries.

On my second screen, an alert went off for $100. I had my

character crouch in the corner while I read the donation, which said it was private, to be read off-stream: "PICK UP YOUR PHONE, ERIC! NOW!" from Just-in-time.

Freaking Justin. Persistent as all get out. Hang on. How did he know it was me?

I quickly told my chat I'd be back, muted my stream, and grabbed my phone as I headed for my bedroom. It started buzzing again. My hands shook. My gut told me something was seriously wrong.

"What's going on? Are you okay?" I asked Justin before he could say anything.

"Nice to speak to you too *friend.*" I winced. I deserved that. "I'm fine, but I'm surprised you care." Yes, I deserved that too; I had only been ignoring the guy for the past two and a half years. Despite that, it was good to hear his voice. It sounded like home.

"Justin, what's going on? How did you find my stream? How did you know?"

"Everyone knows. Every. One." His voice was sharp. "It's about to hit the fan, and I figured you'd want a friend."

"What do you mean?" I paced around my bedroom.

"You've been doxxed. Hacked. Some random dude got ahold of your name and address somehow and posted it online. Your address on your account is still your old one in Colorado, and some ESPN e-sports broadcaster put two and two together. They came pounding on my door, so to speak, looking for you."

"What did you tell them?"

"They asked me about you streaming as EHucker, and I denied it. I had no idea you streamed anyway. I was as surprised as you are now. You haven't picked up your phone in ages. The only way I knew you were alive was from Emily. So listen, the way these things go, it's a matter of time before they post an article and out you. I figured I better warn you."

"How did this happen?" I asked more to myself than him.

Of course, my stream had been losing followers since I chose to not reveal myself. I didn't realize what a big deal it would be until afterward. Still, I got back on the hamster wheel and kept my stream running, thinking no one knew who I was except my family and Jenna...

"I'm sorry, man. The article just popped up."

A moment later, my phone buzzed with a link from Justin, and I read it out loud.

"EHucker360 Revealed as Former Snowboarder Eric Slayter.

"Eric Slayter, twenty-five, has been revealed as the anonymous gamer and streamer EHucker360 on Simmerz, a popular streaming website. Slayter was a brand-new pro snowboarder with a bright future when an injury ended his career. Since then, he's been MIA but apparently has been building a new career as the mysterious EHucker360.

"We reached out to his best friend, Justin Roth, who was unaware of Slayter's stream. Our anonymous source says Slayter has been spending a lot of time at the arcade bar Button Mashers, in Indiana. We hope to catch up with him soon to get all the details."

The article continued on from there, talking about the gaming and streaming industry and how streaming as a career was rare since the market was so saturated.

I tried not to hyperventilate. Did Jenna tell? To include where I've been hanging out means it wasn't some anonymous hacker; it was someone I knew. My parents didn't know how to look up my stream, they just knew I was a streamer, and Emily had been on my stream, but she would never. That only leaves Jenna. Maybe she told Lewis, or Bryan and Alyssa, and one of them let it slip. But why? Ever since meeting the face cam goal, she kept pushing me to stop hiding. Ultimately, even if she didn't go running to the press directly, she still told the secret I was desperate to keep.

My stomach churned. "Justin, I have to go."

"I'm here if you need me, brother."

I stumbled back into my office to find out my character was now dead. My real name scrolled through the chat. Moderators did what they could to control it by switching to subscriber mode, but that didn't make a difference.

Now everyone knew. They chattered on about my looks and my identity. They even found the link to the video of my fall. It was buried deep, but nothing's ever completely gone on the internet. Some people were elated to find out I was a former pro snowboarder and not just some nobody—they were going wild.

I shut off my stream without saying a word. Pain ripped through my chest. She betrayed me. Whether she knew it or not. I trusted her.

I grabbed my phone and hit her number. She picked up after two rings.

"Hey, hot stuff. I'm at Button Mashers." I heard a guy's voice in the background. "Lewis says hi."

"Who did you tell?"

"Huh? What are you talking about?"

"About me! About EHucker and my stream!" I pulled at my hair. I meant to ask her calmly, but darkness had burst through, ready to kill any happiness I had gained.

"*I* didn't. What are you talking about? Who knows about it?"

"EVERYONE!" I roared at her. "Everyone knows, Jenna! All of ESPN, all of my chat. Do I need to spell it out? Ev-er-y-one! It was the one thing I trusted you with!"

"Eric..." she whispered, then a quivering voice: "I didn't. I don't know how... Let me help you. Let me help you figure this out."

"No, Jenna." My voice was hard, and I no longer recognized it. "No. We're done."

I hung up the phone and tossed it onto my pillow. I ran to the bathroom and threw up everything I had for dinner. Sitting on the floor, I put my head between my knees and tried to breathe. I pushed the shower curtain back and rolled myself into the tub, fully clothed. I reached up and turned the knob to the coldest setting. Icy water poured over me, soaking my clothes and making them stick to my skin.

When I finally felt like I could breathe again, I turned off the shower, peeled off my clothes, and climbed into bed. The sting of my anguish and everything I had said to Jenna hit me all at once. I pushed the guilt aside. Darkness, my new friend, diluted its harsh edges. I now welcomed it in.

No more light for me.

Chapter Twenty-Three

JENNA

My hand trembled as I did a search for EHucker on my phone. An article posted fifteen minutes ago revealed Eric's identity and mentioned Button Mashers. I scanned it then dropped my phone on the bar.

"Jenna?"

"Lewis," I whispered.

He grabbed my phone and read the article.

"I didn't... I swear... He just... Eric... said it was over." I was visibly shaking now and unable to focus. Was this anything like what Eric felt?

Lewis hauled me off my bar seat. I didn't even see him come around the bar. He grabbed my purse and phone, then led me outside, leaving the other bartender to cover for him.

Once we made it around the corner, I collapsed against the wall. Lewis knelt in front of me.

"He's EHucker? What did he say to you?"

"He blames me. He thinks I told someone, or the reporters. All his chat knows and—oh no! Lewis, they're going to come here. The reporters are going to come here looking for him!"

I burst into tears. Lewis pulled me to his chest and held me.

"He said it was over. I didn't... I wouldn't... Why would he think?" I blubbered mindlessly.

"Shh." He gently stroked my back trying to comfort me. "Let me take you home."

"I don't want to be alone."

"Don't worry. I got you." Lewis quickly tapped out a text and led me to his car.

By the time we arrived at my house, I had calmed down a bit. Lewis followed me in and made himself at home on my couch.

"I'm sorry, Lewis. I'll be fine. You can go. I'm going to go to bed," I said, wiping another tear.

"Nope." He patted the spot next to him. "Feel free to change and get comfortable. I'm not going anywhere."

"Lewis..."

"Jenna. That idiot broke your heart. I'm here for you. Reinforcements will be here soon."

"Reinforcements?"

"Alyssa and Bryan. I texted them. Alyssa's staying over. Bryan is picking up Insomnia Cookies and some ice cream. Now get over here."

His thoughtfulness had me tearing up again. I relented and joined him on the couch. Lewis tucked me under his arm, and I cried on his chest.

"Thank you. For being here for me." I sat up, grabbed the blanket off the back of the couch, and wrapped it around me.

"How long have you known?" he asked.

"Since I revealed myself at the last tournament. He told me then."

Lewis sucked in a breath.

"I forgave him for lying because I care about him. It also made sense why I always clicked with EHucker. I couldn't fault him for being secretive—that was what I did. He asked me not to tell anyone and I didn't, but I did encourage him to be himself, because it was so freeing for me."

"It can't just be because of ESPN wanting to find him. That would blow over soon enough."

"It's not. He's... holding on to something. He's not forgiving himself."

Lewis sat back and laced his fingers behind his head. "Yeah, I can see that. Maybe you can help him."

"He doesn't want me." I dropped my head into my hands, sobbing yet again.

"I don't know if that's the case, Jenna. Even so, I think he *needs* you right now."

I lifted my head up. "Too bad."

"You don't mean that."

I took a shuddering breath. "I know. I need time."

I got up and went to blow my nose in the restroom. I splashed some water on my face and then took the box of tissues with me back to the couch, just in case.

Trying to take my mind off Eric, I asked, "So has that woman, Ella, been back to the bar yet?"

Lewis ran his hand down his face and sighed. "No. Haven't seen her."

"Really? I was sure she'd be back. Maybe she'll swing by."

"I have her drink ready."

"What do you mean?"

"Her drink. The Moscow mule. I've procured the ingredients. I've even bought fresh mint every week."

"Wow. She really left an impression."

"Something like that," he muttered.

A knock sounded at the door, and I opened it to find Bryan and Alyssa.

"Oh my gosh, Jenna! What happened? I came as quickly as I could. Lewis texted that it was urgent and to bring my overnight bag, Bryan, and sweets."

Bryan held a white-and-purple Insomnia box and a Ben and Jerry's container. "Cookies are still hot."

Once they were inside, Lewis stood up from the couch to say hi.

I texted them the link to the article. After a minute, they both looked up and just stared at me, mouths ajar.

"Are you freaking kidding me?" she said. "Your internet dude and Eric are one and the same?"

"That's not the bad part," Lewis said.

"I've known for a while now, but I was keeping his secret. He thinks I told reporters. He broke up with me." The tears I thought I had kept at bay started welling up.

"Oh, sweetie!" Alyssa pulled me into a hug, and I cried on her shoulder.

"I'll get the spoons," Bryan said.

"It looks like you're in good hands," said Lewis. "I need to head back to the bar to close out. Call me if you need anything, Jenna. Seriously."

I pulled back from Alyssa and hugged Lewis. He kissed me on top of my head. I thanked him again and he left.

Bryan returned with a warm, extra-large s'more cookie topped with cookie dough ice cream. I took a bite, and it melted on my tongue. They dug into theirs too.

We curled up on the couch, and I told them everything that happened with Eric, from when I found out he was EHucker to when he called me tonight, blaming me for leaking his info.

"Wait. I don't understand. Why is it a big deal if people know who he is?" Alyssa asked.

"I guess the media harassed him and his family after his injury. I think because he couldn't snowboard anymore." I shoved a spoonful of ice cream and a bite of cookie in my mouth.

"Well, we know you didn't say anything. So who could have?" Alyssa asked.

I shrugged. That was the least of my concerns right now.

"You've been quiet," Alyssa said, nudging Bryan.

Finished with his dessert, Bryan set down his dish on the coffee table. "What are you going to do now?"

"Bryan, I don't think—"

He put his hand on Alyssa's knee, gently quieting her. Bryan always approached things from a rational angle. Now that the initial shock had worn off, I was ready to hear his thoughts.

"What are you going to do, Jenna?"

"I don't know, Bryan. I guess try to get over it somehow. Move on." My lip trembled as I fought back tears.

"Screw that."

My mouth fell open.

"You love him," he said. "I've seen it in your eyes. I know that look because it's the same one I see Alyssa have for me. It sounds to me like Eric is lost. And I know you were lost not so long ago."

"It's not the same," I said.

"It's not. We knew you were fighting against your fears all along. But we also knew you wouldn't stay undercover forever—you were meant to game with the best. One day you'd find the strength to overcome all of that. Eric...? I don't know if he knows where to start. You seem to be the first person he's let in on his secret. I don't think you're prepared to give up on him. He helped you see your worth. Now I think he needs help seeing his."

Alyssa and I stared at Bryan in shock. He was right about all of it.

Bryan stood up. "I'm going to head out. Take your time, Jenna. But not too long." With that, Bryan kissed Alyssa goodbye and left. We watched the door shut behind him.

"That... that beautiful man is right." Alyssa sighed. I could almost see the little hearts in her eyes.

I brushed away a rouge tear. "I know." Freaking Bryan. Always full of wisdom.

From the beginning, my friends saw the pain Eric was holding on to. They were right; he did need me. But first, I was going to wallow a bit longer.

"Rom-com marathon?" I asked Alyssa.

"Let's do it."

With our desserts finished and bowls set aside, we popped in

The Wedding Date after putting on our pajamas and spent the rest of the evening binging movies and talking, until Alyssa fell asleep.

I lay in bed restless, thinking of all the possibilities of what could have happened. Ever since he received those drop-ins and reached his face cam goal, things had been strange. And now this? Knowing about Button Mashers? Someone was behind this, and I was more determined than ever to figure it out.

Because I was going to fight for Eric. Especially if he couldn't fight for himself.

Chapter Twenty-Four

ERIC

The sun sneaking in through my bedroom blinds woke me. I threw my arm over my eyes and groaned.

A week had passed since my identity was revealed, and I hadn't left my apartment. My stream remained off, and after two days of constant messages and social media pings, I shut down my phone. I only texted Emily to assure her that I was okay. I don't know if she believed me, but if she saw me now, she'd be doing everything to pull me back together.

Jenna's silence was deafening but expected; I yelled at her. My mind would only let me believe that she was lying or else she would have called to explain herself.

She did. You didn't give her a chance.

I brushed that thought aside. The growl of my stomach pulled me from my bed to the kitchen. I opened the cabinets and found a half-eaten bag of chips and an expired can of soup. The empty cabinets were a reminder that I wasn't caring for my basic needs.

Pizza it is.

I powered up my phone and winced at the onslaught of missed calls and messages. I nearly choked on my own saliva after seeing I had thousands of notifications on my socials. I pulled up the app for the pizza place. But before I could select anything, someone pounded on my door.

I couldn't move. Last week, Bryan and Lewis pounded on my door, but I had ignored them. Maybe they were back. Or could it be the media?

"Open the door, Eric!"

That voice. What was he doing here?

Without a thought, I swung the door open and pulled Justin inside.

Big, blond, and broad-shouldered, he all but filled up my living room. His emerald-colored eyes trailed around my apartment before landing on me.

"Are you crazy?" I shouted.

"Hello to you too."

"Did anyone follow you?"

"Are you kidding me? No, dude. Relax," he said, clapping a hand on my shoulder. "You're an ex-snowboarder, not the next MJ."

"Michael Jackson or Michael Jordan?"

"Either. Look, I'm supposed to be on the slopes tomorrow. I left those ESPN reporters in Colorado. What in the world Eric?" he asked, waving his hand around my apartment. "What happened here?"

The result of ignoring everything around me for a week showed: Take-out containers were piled up high out of my trash and dishes sat dirty in the sink. This wasn't like me; even if I wasn't organized, I always kept my place clean and tidy.

"Why are you here?" I asked.

Justin crossed his arms and stepped closer so that he was in my face. "I could punch you right now. Like, knock you out."

"Good. Do it," I challenged. "Give me some reprieve."

I stumbled sideways after a hand whacked me across the head, hard enough to hurt. "What was that for!"

"I thought you wanted me to hit you."

"I thought you were going to punch me, not smack me in the head!"

"I wanted you to snap out of it. I should have visited long before now. We need to have a serious talk. But first, go shower. You reek. When you're done, get your butt back out here and help me clean up this dump."

Justin sauntered into my kitchen. He put all his weight on the trash to compress it, lifted it out, and tied it up. Next he opened my utility closet, found a new bag, and started chucking in the garbage from the floor. How he knew exactly where I kept my trash bags, I had no idea.

I missed the guy. I hadn't realized until this moment how much I needed his friendship. I couldn't believe he was here. His presence alone jolted me out of the fog I was living in.

He looked up to catch me staring. "Now!" he ordered.

I retreated to my bathroom, where I washed off a week's worth of odor in the shower. Then I pulled on some jeans and a t-shirt and joined him in the kitchen.

Justin stood at the sink, rinsing off dirty dishes. Then he placed them in the dishwasher.

"Thanks, honey," I teased.

He spun around and pulled me into a hug. "Now that you don't smell like a dead rat, I can greet you properly." He patted me on the back before stepping back. "Anywhere we can grab a drink?"

"I don't know…"

"Dude. It's fine. We are getting out of this apartment."

"Okay," I said, suddenly tired of these four walls. "I know a taco place. I'm starving." I grabbed my keys.

"Tacos? Say no more."

We arrived at Walko Taco, the place Lewis and I had gone after Ultimate Frisbee. We ordered a platter of street tacos and a couple of beers. I wasn't ready to talk, so Justin caught me up on his life instead.

His snowboarding career had taken off. It was something we always dreamed about doing together. After consistently winning competitions, he gained a steady stream of sponsorships and support. He was even in a couple of commercials.

My heart hurt with the loss of what we could have had together, yet I was also very happy for Justin. There was no reconciling the warring emotions right now.

Justin had met a woman at a new bakery in his town. "So I've had to watch my weight and up my workouts ever since," Justin said, patting his flat stomach. He was lured in by an amazingly decorated cake in the store window, but it was her brownies that hooked him. "That cake was freaking artwork. But when that warm gooey chocolate hit my taste buds, I was done for." Justin had found his weakness.

"She sounds awesome."

"She really is. We've only been on two dates. I don't know if it'll work out though."

"Why not?"

He shrugged and turned his head. He was hiding something. I got it; I wasn't privy to all his thoughts anymore. In some ways it was weird talking with Justin again, but in other ways, it was the most natural thing, like we had never been apart.

"Look Justin, I'm sorry—"

Justin held up his hand. "No, Eric. None of that. I'm not here to guilt-trip you or make you feel bad. Yes, I came in kind of hot, but that's only because I care about you. You were—you *are* a terrible mess. As I said, I should have shown up way earlier. Part of me hoped if I gave you space, you would find your own way out of it. I assumed you were busy working some job here. I had no clue you were a famous streamer. That's wild." He made a motion with his hands like his mind was blown.

"Shh!" It was bad enough the world knew about me; I didn't need my local taco bar knowing too.

"Bro, we're fine." He scooped another taco off the platter and downed half of it in one bite.

"It just sort of happened," I told him.

"Okay, so maybe you had some luck, but those things don't just happen. It takes some level of dedication and persistence on your part. And I know where you got that work ethic. Emily told me you have thousands of viewers every stream. The question is, why hide all this time? And what's going on with that woman?"

"What did Emily tell you?" I asked, gritting my teeth.

"Dang. Chill. We still talk. Just because you cut me out doesn't mean I abandoned your sister. I grew up with her too."

I ran my hands through my hair. "I know. You're right. I'm sorry."

"Talk to me," Justin said.

"I don't know where to start."

Justin waved the server over and ordered two more beers. "Start at the beginning."

Chapter Twenty-Five

JENNA

I watched mindlessly as the ghosts chased Ms. PacMan around the board, moving the joystick to outmaneuver each of them. She gobbled up all the dots, and the next board loaded.

"Jenna?"

I wondered how Eric was doing. How could I find out who told everyone, and when I did, would he believe me?

"Jenna..."

He never used his gamertag name or said anything about gaming while here. Who at Button Mashers would have connected Eric to EHucker?

"Jenna!"

I jumped, knocking the joystick the wrong way, and finally Ms. PacMan died from the unrelenting ghosts.

I turned to Lewis on my right.

"Are you okay?" he asked, his voice low.

"Yeah. I'm fine. Why?"

"Your eyes haven't left the screen in an hour."

Just then, my score loaded.

"Woah Jenna, that's the highest score I've ever seen on one of these machines."

I shrugged.

"The last tournament is tonight. Are you going to play?"

"Yes, of course," I said, affronted by the thought of him even questioning it.

Lewis glanced at the bar. More people were arriving now for tournament night, and his other bartenders were bustling around the bar, getting everyone their drinks. Lewis nodded toward the bar. "Come on. Come sit."

As I followed him, a few of the regular competitors waved at me. For the most part, everyone was friendly after discovering I was Jenson, but I hadn't figured out where I fit in with the group after being someone else for so long.

Once Lewis got the bar caught up, he passed me a water and leaned in.

"Have you spoken to Eric?"

"No. He won't answer my calls."

Lewis shook his head. He was as upset about what happened with Eric as I was. He even tried to go to his apartment to get him to talk but was only met with silence.

"Who do you think figured it out?" I said. "It wasn't me, and I know it wasn't you or my friends. It could have been a random internet hacker who got into his account, but the fact that they knew about this place—it has to be someone from here."

Lewis scratched his chin. "You're right. That crossed my mind too. But we can't go around accusing people."

"But how do we find out?"

"I think we need to keep our ears and eyes open."

"You're probably right." I sighed, resting my chin in my hand.

I mindlessly scrolled through my phone, checking my socials and then email. "Oh my gosh!" I squealed, quickly scanning the email again.

"What?" Lewis asked, looking alarmed.

"I made it! I made it into SimmerzCon!"

"Congrats Jenna!" He made his way around the bar and lifted me into a hug. "I knew you were a shoo-in."

"Thanks. I'll be teamed up with Trekster and TakeNote. I guess they requested me as their teammate."

Suddenly Lewis flew back around the bar and, keeping his head low, began to mix a cocktail. I didn't understand what was wrong until I turned around. Ella, the woman Lewis had gotten special drink ingredients for, stood by the door. A man in a dress shirt and tie had placed his hand on her back. Were they on a date? She stared at Lewis, and I thought I saw hurt flash across her face then disappear. Did she see him hugging me? She said something to the man and marched up to the bar.

Lewis looked up and held out a drink for her. Her special drink. It was her Moscow Mule in a copper mug, a slice of lime on the ledge and mint leaves garnishing the top. Her eyes widened. I waited to see what would happen next, but she just paid, said "Thank you," and rejoined her date at an arcade game.

Lewis watched her go, looking confused. But then more customers arrived, and he got back to work. A few college girls found seats at the bar and started flirting with Lewis, laughing and batting their eyelashes. While he typically enjoyed the attention, he didn't have much of a reaction tonight. I looked back over at Ella in the arcade. She seemed like she was having fun, but she kept stealing glances at Lewis.

Interesting.

"Yo, Jenna."

Henry, or gamertag Lockout, slid into the seat next to me. I had taken him up on his invitation and played some matches with him and his friends online. We had fun and built a friendly rapport.

"How's it going?" Henry asked now.

"Good. Actually, I just found out I'm going to SimmerzCon!"

"Really? That's amazing. But it's not surprising. You deserve it."

"Thank you."

"Sit in my seat for the tournament."

"What?"

"Sit in my seat. Toward the middle. I'll take the corner spot," he said, smiling.

I looked in that direction and lightly bit my lip. "I don't know..."

"It'll be great. I was talking to the other guys, and they all want to watch you play. We've only seen the results of a Jenson win, but no one has seen it live."

My stomach flipped over. Yes, there was some nervousness, but I was also excited. Ever since I faced my fears, gaming was easier and even more enjoyable than before. I was slowly finding communities that I fit into and people I enjoyed playing with. No one mentioned the video, and I would have forgotten about it except for Carter and his friends whispering "Trained girl" when I passed by.

"I'll think about it."

Henry gave me a knowing smile. "Sure. I'll see you in a bit." He got up and went back to his friends at the consoles.

Suddenly, a pair of arms snaked around my waist.

"Surprise," Alyssa said.

I turned to also find Bryan, Trekster, and TakeNote. "What are you doing here?"

"We're here for the final Button Mashers tournament of course. And to see our best friend kick some booty."

My throat tightened as I was overcome with emotion. Everyone was here. Except Eric.

"We wanted to support our teammate," said Trekster.

TakeNote nodded and flashed me a smile. "I've been excited all week for this!"

"Have you heard from him?" I asked Trekster.

"Sorry, Jenna. From what I can tell, he hasn't been online, so he likely hasn't read my messages."

Bryan stepped forward. "We'll figure it out. For now, we're here. Go have fun."

I nodded, grateful for my friends. Without them, without Eric... I would still be Jenson. And my dream of going to SimmerzCon would be impossible because I couldn't enter under my gamertag alone. My brother would have loved this. He would have been at every tournament, cheering me on or even competing against me to make me better.

"Okay. I'm ready."

Henry was standing at his seat. I walked over and synced my controller to the system and plugged in my headset. Carter sat two chairs over, looking displeased with the new seating arrangement. Before I could change my mind, Henry stepped to my side, blocking Carter's view.

"Ignore him," Henry said.

"Aren't you going to compete?"

"Nah. I decided I want to watch your game tonight."

I smiled. It felt unreal—refreshing—to have such support. I almost didn't care if I won or lost tonight; I was already having the best time.

I put on my headset, ready for the tournament to begin.

Chapter Twenty-Six

ERIC

Three Years Ago

My board tipped over the edge of the slope, and I glided into the half-pipe. The wind pressed against me, making balance a bit more challenging than usual. I've practiced in a blizzard with low visibility, and in freezing sleet before, so this did not faze me. Adrenaline took over as I drove up the far side of the pipe. I launched into my first trick and landed solidly. The faint roar of the cheering crowd met my ears and my confidence grew. I successfully landed my last trick, the pretzel, and glided to a stop at the bottom of the slope and waited.

After a long moment, my scores blasted through the PA system: "85, 83, 87!"

I pumped my fist in the air. That placed me right behind Justin. I was determined to beat him. Nothing wrong with some friendly competition between two men who were practically brothers. We trained together almost every day, and our families were close. However, that wouldn't stop me from taking the win from him tonight. He didn't know what was coming.

"Nice run, bro!" he said, fist-bumping me as I prepared to head back up the mountain.

"Thanks, but your newbie moves are not going to stand up to my next run. I'm about to sweep this whole competition." I smirked.

Justin laughed. "Yeah whatever, Hucker." I was dubbed the nickname by my snowboarding peers after they watched me perform some wild tricks on the half-pipe. It was a term for someone who was reckless in the air. Tonight was no exception. Justin glanced over my shoulder. "Incoming."

I was jostled forward as two arms wrapped around my waist. I turned around to find my girlfriend, Kara, in layers and layers of snow gear. She was so bundled up she looked like a puffball with two eyes peeking out.

"I'm soooo cold! I cannot wait until your last run is over so we can head inside." She nuzzled my neck. "Mmm, but you are soooo warm."

Justin rolled his eyes behind her back I felt the same. I returned the hug, appreciating her body pressed against mine.

We'd been dating for nine months, and we got along well enough. I got annoyed by her complaining but learned to tune it out. She didn't appreciate my craft and hated the cold.

"Babe, I need to focus and head up the mountain again." I kissed her on the forehead and turned toward the half-pipe.

"Fine. I hope my limbs don't turn to ice and break off."

I resisted rolling my eyes yet again. "I promise we'll do whatever you want tonight. Just you and me and no snowboard talk." Ideally, there wouldn't be any talking at all.

"Promise?"

"Promise." I knew I'd regret it if we ended up watching another chick flick, but at least she was here. That was more than some of the snowboarders could say about their significant others.

By the time I'm released from Kara's arms, I had to scurry up the hill, feeling a bit more flustered than usual. I allowed myself to get distracted and now my run would start any minute. I closed my eyes and envisioned my routine. I made a special note to visualize my last trick. I've pulled off 95 percent of it before, but I needed everything to be perfect for the last element. I could easily beat Justin if I aced it, and today I would.

I tipped my board forward over the lip of the slope and zoomed down toward the half-pipe. I completed my first two tricks flawlessly, a backside 540 and a crippler. I advanced down the pipe, gaining speed for my final trick. The one I was almost completely confident about. A frontside double cork 1080. I launched myself into the air and started rotating but then I was caught by the wind and my body weight shifted. I flailed then slam down on the edge of the pipe, flipped off the top and slid to the ground.

Pain. Pain was everywhere. Then the world went black.

Sleep, eat, video games, physical therapy, repeat. That was what my life had become. Six months after my fall, a press release went out last week by my team, my career as a snowboarder was over. My knee would never recover completely, and it would be too easy to injure myself again. My shoulder fared better, but the scars would remain.

Immediately Kara dumped me with a text. Whatever.

Justin invited me out to watch him practice, but it hurt too much. Watching him made me yearn to be out there.

The worst was when all my sponsorships dropped me, because now my parents were scrambling to figure out what to do. Their lives were dependent on what my sponsorships provided—my dad was my coach, and my mom worked only part-time at a preschool only to keep herself busy. They've supported my snowboarding since I was young, giving me everything I needed to be successful. As a professional, it was my turn to return the favor.

But now I had nothing.

Playing games and watching streams were my only reprieve. I moderated for a streamer named Trekster when I could at night. Been watching him since the start. Recently his stream had grown a lot. We'd become pretty good friends through the years. It looked like I'd have plenty of time to help him out.

I decided to message him.

EHucker360: Game?

Trekster: Dude, it's the middle of the day! What are you doing online?

EHucker360: I'll explain everything while we play.

I opened the game and got on voice chat with him. I ended up telling him almost everything. That I lost my dream career because of an injury and how I was not sure what to do next or how I'd pay my medical bills.

"You're a personable guy," Trekster said. "You should start streaming. There's a bit of setup and you really have to grind at it, but I bet you could make a little cash doing it."

I thought about what he said but started researching other jobs. But it proved difficult to find one that worked with my rigorous physical therapy schedule. Finally, I tried streaming, but I didn't want to be in the spotlight.

I devised a plan: If I managed to acquire a big enough following, I'd show myself on camera. But I'd make my face cam goal so high it'd be impossible to achieve. No one could know that I was Eric Slayter.

EHucker360: Okay, I'm going to start streaming. But I want to build my own community. I don't want to play with you on stream or have you give me a shout-out until I build my own following.

Trekster: All right, man! That's respectable. I'll support you behind the scenes for now.

EHucker360: Thank you.

I spent the next two days setting up my channel for my very first stream.

"We're moving where?" I yelled.

"Sweetie, you know my family is back in Indiana. I want to be close to them again," Mom said.

"Why? Why now? Is it because I can't snowboard anymore?"

Mom eyed Dad and lowered her head. I couldn't see Emily, but I suspected she was listening from the stairs.

"I know it's been a rough year for you, Eric, but your mother and I can't afford this house anymore. We tried to make it work. It's just not panning out. Of course, you're twenty-three, and you're welcome to get an apartment and stay here. You'll have to find a job, but you're perfectly capable. You can find something."

"So that's it? I screw up my career, and you bail on me?"

"That's not what's happening. We always intended to move closer to family," he said. "But we wanted to be here and support your dream."

"Sorry I held you back all this time." In a way this was worse than my injury, knowing my dream messed up my parents' lives.

"Eric, let me be clear," my dad said, moving to stand in front of me. He placed his hand on my good shoulder. "This has been our home. We love living here. But life is never quite what we plan it to be. We would have stayed another ten years if things were different. I'm sorry, son. I'm so sorry. Life dealt you a poor hand this time, and you must figure out what to do next. You have to keep moving forward."

A realization hit me: I was the sole cause of this shift. There was no moving forward for me, not until I could fix things. If it wasn't for my arrogance, if I would have practiced that trick 5% more to really master it, I wouldn't have fallen. I'd still be out on the slopes, Mom would be planning her next dinner party, Dad would be coaching me, and Emily would be pirouetting on stage. I screwed up everything for my whole family. I would make up for it and until then, I wouldn't forgive myself.

"I'll go with you," I declared.

Mom perked up. "You will?"

"Yes. There's nothing else for me here. I want to be there for Emily and you guys. I'll get an apartment in Indiana. I need to figure some things out for myself."

"What about Justin?" Emily asked, peeking around the corner.

I turned around to face her. With her pouty lips and creased brows, she looked like someone had sat on her birthday cake. She was fifteen and right in that awkward boy-crazy phase. She had known him for as long as she had known me. It would be hard for her to say goodbye. Despite her feelings, I couldn't think about him.

"He'll be fine. He'll have the dream pro career like he's always wanted. He doesn't need me to pull him down. Excuse me. There's something I have to do." I grabbed my crutches and hobbled out of the kitchen.

I had discussed a tattoo design with an artist in town. It was time to go get it. I would leave the mountains behind, but in this way, I would also take them with me.

To remember and to forget.

Chapter Twenty-Seven

JENNA

Button Mashers was buzzing. I sat in Henry's seat and tried to ignore the people who had gathered behind me, including Alyssa, Bryan, TakeNote, and Trekster. I took a deep breath.

The first match went quickly. I played an average game but still made it onto the scoreboard, right below Carter. For the next one, I was warmed up, and I won.

After two more games, it was time for the final one, the most challenging of the evening. I narrowly avoided death, thankful for the revive I bought. In the end, Carter and I had the last characters on the map.

He had the high ground, and I snuck below. Luckily the circle pulled toward me, and he had to jump down. He aimed his gun at me, but I hit him with a stun. That disoriented him enough for me to shoot him down and win the game.

Cheers erupted around me. I smiled and removed my headset. My friends circled around and congratulated me.

When everyone finally calmed down, I packed up my bag and set it under my seat. I stepped away to use the restroom—this time to actually use it, not to change out of a disguise. When I came back to my station to grab my bag, Carter approached me.

"You know, I've been thinking. It's hot that you play video games. And your ex, he's an idiot."

I raised an eyebrow, surprised at his statement. Not that it made me like him any, but still.

Carter moved close and snaked an arm around my waist. I felt his hot breath on my ear, and he whispered, "I'd train you better."

I twisted and pushed him back by the shoulders. He stumbled backward, smirking.

Shocked, I scanned the bar for my friends: nowhere in sight. They were probably there with Lewis, waiting for me, but there were too many people obstructing my view.

"Oh, come on, Jenna. Don't be shy. I'll treat you better than that other guy. Where is he anyway?" He glanced over his shoulder.

"Who?"

"Don't play dumb—Eric."

"Not here." I tried to step around him, but he blocked me again. I was always wary of Carter, but now I had to ignore the fear swirling inside.

"Tsk. Well, since your little streamer boyfriend has abandoned you, come over, baby. We can take a break from video games, and I'll let you play with me." He grabbed at me, but I stepped aside.

"What did you say?"

"I can show you a real good time."

"No. Before that," I demanded.

"About your streamer boyfriend? EHucker is it? Yeah, I know about him. Eric Slayter. EHucker. Loser ex-snowboarder with a bum knee."

My mouth dropped open. Carter was the one who had figured it out. He was the reason for Eric's misery.

"How did you find out? And why do you care?"

Carter crossed his arms. "That was easy. I didn't get what you saw in the guy, so I dug around and found out he was a pro snowboarder. Then I heard you chatting away with Trekster and that other chick about some EHucker guy."

I rolled my eyes. Of course, he would know Trekster and not TakeNote.

"I'm something of a computer whiz, so for fun, I hacked EHucker, and to my surprise, he's Eric. I don't know why he streams secretly, but I figured it was high time he showed everyone what a loser he truly is. So I had a few streamers drop in to meet his face cam goal."

"You sent those streamers his way?" I cried.

Carter shrugged. "When he didn't reveal himself, I had to reach out to some old buddies to get that article published."

"Why? Why did you do all that?"

"Because you've always blown me off. You ignored every guy in here until *he* showed up and then suddenly, we find out you're the one beating all of us. A girl who is just an internet joke."

That hurt. He was exactly the type of person I was trying to avoid by disguising myself. But today, I would not back down.

"You're the only one who thinks that, Carter. I've moved on, everyone else here has moved on." I waved to the small circle of people that were listening in. "And as for Eric, leave him alone. He has nothing to do with this. I would never date you, even if I had no other options."

Carter laughed. He leaned in even closer. "Eric is a trash video-game player, and you know it."

I no longer felt the fear; my blood was boiling. Before I could react, Carter was hauled away by someone gripping his collar. A tall, muscular man stood over Carter.

"If I ever hear you speak badly about Eric again, I will plow my fist into your face!"

Oh wow. The guy looked somewhat familiar, but I couldn't quite place him.

"Who the heck are you?" Carter squeaked.

"Eric's best friend. And I suggest you keep your mouth shut about him."

Justin? That's right—I had seen him in one of Eric's photos. What was he doing here? That's when I noticed Eric, standing nearby looking utterly lost and conflicted.

"All right. Break it up!" Lewis barked, stepping in.

Carter scoffed and shoved Justin. "Ah, failed snowboarder,

outcast streamer, come to grace our presence at good ol' Button Mashers." Carter moved closer to Eric. "How does it feel to suck at everything you do?"

Instead of making Eric angry, I could see there was even more defeat in his eyes.

"That's it, Carter," said Lewis. "I don't want to hear anything else from you. Either have a drink and leave everyone alone, or get out. Make a wise decision."

"I think I'll stick around for the show."

Lewis raised a questioning brow, but Carter shrugged and moved toward the bar with his posse.

Justin went after Eric, who had turned to leave. But the front door opened, and that's when things really went downhill.

Chapter Twenty-Eight

ERIC

My head pounded when I woke up from my nap. The extra beers I drank while telling Justin my story hit me hard. I used the bathroom then dragged myself into the kitchen to get some Tylenol, but I didn't see Justin on the couch. I checked my office too, but he was nowhere in sight.

Finally, I found a note by a diffuser that was spewing some floral scent. (What was that about?)

Going to meet the famous Jenna at Button Mashers. Come join me.
—Justin

I'd mentioned to Justin that tonight was the final tournament at Button Mashers and that Jenna would probably be there competing. I suddenly panicked at the thought of him telling her about the state I've been in.

I grabbed my keys and ran out the door.

When I arrived at Button Mashers, I saw a crowd around one of the stations. I looked up to the scoring screen: The tournament was over and Jenna won. I didn't see Justin, and Jenna was not at her normal corner spot. I moved closer to the mass of onlookers.

Carter stood there, talking to someone. I stopped dead when I heard a familiar voice: "And as for Eric, leave him alone. He has nothing to do with this. I would never date you, even if I had no other options."

Carter laughed and leaned in even closer, speaking loud enough that everyone could hear him. "Eric is a trash video-game player, and you know it."

Before I could move in to help, someone pulled Carter away from her. That's when I met Jenna's eyes. And I saw all the love she still had for me, but all I could think was how I had ruined it. Carter was the problem, and I was an idiot. Too blind in my fear and anger to recognize the truth. Would she ever forgive me?

Then Carter turned to me and unloaded his disdain.

He was right. I was all those things. I couldn't take back how I handled everything. Shame washed over me. Lewis gave him a choice to behave or leave. Carter walked away, mentioning something about a show.

I turned to leave, but the door opened and a group poured in. They spotted me immediately and surrounded me where I stood, pushing Justin back. Jenna made her way through the crowd as Lewis tried to call order to the chaos.

I was stuck with no way to escape. Mics were shoved into my face. Reporters. They asked me questions about why I hid my identity and why I left Colorado. I couldn't answer any of them.

I couldn't breathe.

The walls closed in around me, and I started to feel light-headed. I never passed out from the darkness before. The coldness always allowed me to escape and to numb myself. But I was hot. Too hot. I focused on Jenna as I tried to stay present and figure a way out.

Jenna stumbled forward when she was pushed in the back, and I almost lost it. Then a whistle sounded, and the crowd froze.

"Everybody stop!" Lewis bellowed. "All journalists out unless you're buying something or playing a game. Please do not bother my customers. Regulars, get your drinks and hit up the games."

Surprisingly, the reporters dropped their mics and slowly dispersed, most walking out the door. Carter fist-bumped one of them and gave me a knowing look. This was his doing. The regular patrons moved over to the arcade, and I stood there with Justin, Jenna, Trekster, TakeNote, and Lewis. I breathed deeply, trying to calm myself, but nothing seemed to help.

Justin placed his hand on my shoulder, and the whole group hustled me down the hall to the back, where Jenna and I first met.

I slid down the wall. Justin squatted beside me, and Jenna knelt in front of me, while Lewis, Trekster, and TakeNote stood guard at the end of the hall. I put my head between my knees, trying to breathe.

"That's right, buddy," said Justin. "In and out. In and out."

I felt a delicate, warm hand on my arm. It was enough to have me take one more shuddering breath, and the darkness finally receded.

"Is this your first panic attack?" Justin asked.

"No," I finally admitted.

I thought back to all the times I felt worried and overwhelmed in the past two years. All the times I stood on the balcony in the cold or under the icy water of my shower. It was the darkness then too. But I always had control. I wouldn't let it defeat me.

"How did you know?" I asked Justin.

"A friend of mine has them. Plus, I saw your broken mirror and I wondered if it happened because of one. Mirrors don't just magically break on their own."

I heard Jenna make a soft, whimpering noise, and it killed me.

Humiliation washed over me, and I expected Jenna to move away. To give up. But her hand remained on my arm. I focused on Justin, only able to process one thing at a time.

"Since the accident," I answered. "I didn't realize what was going on at first. I thought I was just reacting to the meds for my knee, but when I went off them, it continued."

Jenna's thumb moved gently across my bicep. Letting me know she was there for me. Listening.

"I figured once I recovered, once I repaid my parents, once I got my life back in order that I would feel better. I was always able to control it before it got too far, except with the mirror."

I looked up and locked eyes with Jenna. And I couldn't stop it.

Tears fell and an overwhelming grief overtook my soul. "I'm sorry, Jenna. I'm sorry. I'm so so sorry." I blubbered on.

Jenna removed her hand and scooted in close, wrapping her arms around me. I cried into her neck as she slowly rubbed my back.

"It's okay, Eric. It'll be okay. I forgive you. I already had."

Hearing those words calmed me and finally brought me back to my senses. I was embarrassed for showing such emotion but also relieved that I was not alone in it for once.

"Thank you. You will never know how much that means to hear that. But how can you forgive me? I messed everything up so badly."

"I love you, Eric. And I will stand by your side and help you through this. But I need you to tell me how."

I shook my head. I didn't earn the generosity and love she was giving me. I pulled back slightly, and the look on her face broke my heart. But I was unable to say the words back at that moment.

"I need time," I said. "I need to figure things out before I can be the man you deserve." I stood up just as Justin made his way back over. He must have walked away to give us some privacy.

Quiet tears rolled down her face. "You are good enough, Eric. You don't have to push me away."

"I know, Jenna. I know. It's only time. Please."

She had to know that if I could, I would not give up a single minute with her. But when I told my story to Justin, I realized I had to face my past before I could fully open my heart.

She nodded solemnly. "I'll be here. When you're ready."

I met her eyes, praying that she would be.

I turned to Justin, who nodded and joined us.

"My car is out back," he said, and we walked out, leaving Jenna behind.

"Not having a mirror in here is really putting a crimp in my daily routine," Justin called from the bathroom. He was using my bathroom since my shower had a taller showerhead than the hall bathroom. He had been in there for over a half hour getting ready.

I still hadn't replaced the mirror, finding it easier to go about my day if I didn't have to look at myself.

I arched a brow, still lying in bed. "Dude, you've been in there forever. What could you possibly be doing?"

"Manscaping," he said in all seriousness.

"Why?" I paused. "You know what? I don't want to know."

Justin let out a laugh. "I like to feel fresh and smooth all around."

"Ah, jeez."

My emotions last night were all over the place and my heart ached at letting Jenna go for now. After a long talk with Justin, I realized the first thing I needed to do was speak with my parents.

Apparently, Justin had some experience with anxiety, what I had been calling my darkness. One of the guys he snowboards with was dealing with it before each competition, something beyond the typical nervousness. He read books on the subject and even talked to a counselor about how he could be a supportive friend and help him through it. That's how he was able to see what I never could in myself.

I rolled out of bed and stood in the bathroom doorway. Justin was now rolling something on his chest. My eyes widened when I saw the little amber glass bottles lining the counter.

"What the heck is all that?"

Justin grinned. "Essential oils. Emily told me about them. This one"—he held up a bottle—"helps me with my breathing when I run." He screwed the cap back on and pointed to his collection. "This one I use as cologne. It smells nice and attracts the ladies— right now that's Rebecca. This one I use for immune support, this I put on my stomach when my digestion is out of whack, and this I diffuse at night to sleep better."

"Diffuse? And *Emily* got you into all this? My sister?"

"Yeah, she started using essential oils to help her muscles for ballet. Anyway, you put a few drops in with some water in a diffuser and breathe in all the oily goodness. Oh! And this one keeps me calm. I put it on my head or wrists. Dude, here, have this bottle. We must get you a diffuser. You know what, forget it, have mine. I have four more at home."

Justin stepped toward me, and before I could stop him, he grabbed my wrist and swiped his roller across.

I jumped back. "Hey! What are you doing?"

"Just relax. Breathe it in," he said while smelling his own wrist.

I slowly lifted my arm and took a whiff. At first, I scrunched up my nose. But then I took another sniff. Not bad. It was a cross between lavender, vanilla, and something else. It was oddly... calming.

"See, I knew you would like it."

He corralled some bottles into a corner, presumably for me to keep and for some reason, I let him, too tired to fight. The rest he put away in a bag that had a slot for each oil.

I sighed. "So what's the plan?"

Justin's face grew serious. "Well, first we're going to your parents' house to see them and Emily and then we will get some groceries on the way home."

"Okay. Let me get cleaned up." I shooed him out of the bathroom and took a shower. I was tempted to turn it to cold but let the warm water rain down on me.

When I was done, I got dressed and grabbed my keys.

We made it out to the parking lot and were suddenly surrounded. The reporters from last night had found us. Everyone yelled things at the same time: "Justin! Eric! How long have you been EHucker? What was your intention for streaming in disguise?"

I couldn't move. Except this time, I had Justin beside me. He took me by the arm and pulled me toward my car.

"How did they find us?" I asked, trying to remain calm.

"Don't know, man. Let's go."

We pushed through the crowd and I veered to the driver's side while Justin went to the passenger's side. I unlocked the doors and we both slid in the car and slammed the doors shut. The reporters were pressed in close to the car, but thankfully had enough sense to step back as I backed out and zoomed out of the lot.

I tried to concentrate on my breathing.

"Do you want to pull over and let me drive?"

I shook my head. "It helps to have a distraction."

We sat quietly as I contemplated my anxiety. I knew something wasn't right with me, but I could never pinpoint it. It was like going down the beginner slope. You know you're descending, but you're moving along so smoothly you don't realize you've hit the bottom. Until you're in the dark.

I pulled into my parents' driveway and cut the engine.

Holding on to the past wasn't healthy. Even if I was able to pay my parents back, it wouldn't ever have been enough to satisfy me. And I was sick of feeling numb.

"Okay. I'm ready to talk."

Justin clapped me on the shoulder. "That's why we're here."

I nodded.

"The first step to healing is realizing you don't have to do it alone. You reach out and talk to your friends." He lifted his chin toward my childhood home. "And your family. I think it'll help."

He was right. I felt a lump in my throat, and climbed out of the car.

That night I stood in my office, staring at my equipment. Everything I had been holding inside I poured out to my family. We had a long talk about everything that transpired in the last couple of years that led us to where we were now, and I finally *heard* my parents when they said they were content. That they didn't care about the sponsorships, the money, the fancy house. They were as happy today as they were before and after my career took off. The only thing they wished was for me to be happy as well.

I couldn't achieve that on the path I was on. The things I was doing and why I was doing them caused my anxiety. It was a big eye-opener to realize that I needed to talk to someone outside of my circle. A therapist could not only help me come to terms with my past but manage my anxiety and look toward the future.

For now, there was one thing I knew I had to do.

I sat down and typed a message to my community. I thanked them all for their support and told them I was taking time off to figure things out.

I closed out of my account, unsure if I would return.

Chapter Twenty-Nine

JENNA

The day I thought would never come had arrived: SimmerzCon. All the time spent practicing and competing was worth it. It felt like I was dreaming as I was handed a special-access pass with my name on one side and my gamertag on the other.

Once I entered the main venue, my mouth dropped open. It was a sight to behold.

Half the room was packed with vendor booths, selling anything and everything that had to do with gaming, from the latest camera technology for streams, to gaming chairs, headsets, and so on. The other half was lined with stations where attendees could try the newest games, many of which were not released yet. The front of the room had chairs and a stage with a huge screen behind it, where a DJ was spinning.

"Wow," I whispered to myself. I scanned the room to see if I recognized anyone. I saw a few familiar streamers but I frowned knowing that the one face I wished to see the most would not be here.

Eric and I had spoken a bit since the last Button Mashers tournament. Our conversations were always light and brief. Though every fiber of my being wanted to be with him and help him, I gave him the time he asked for. I took solace in knowing his family, Justin, and Trekster were always in contact with him.

We were not broken up or on a break. We were more on pause. My heart was still with him. Because I couldn't stand thinking about it and worrying, I filled my time with work and practice. I was as ready as I could be for this tournament.

Shaking off the fact that Eric wasn't with me, I set out toward the merchandise booths.

"This headset is a SimmerzCon exclusive," a salesperson said. "It has Simmerz's official logo and teal color design. You can buy it here today, or we're having a drawing for one later today."

I considered upgrading my headset, so I checked the price—and promptly let out a low whistle. Nope. That was a little above my coffeehouse earnings. I dropped my name in for the drawing instead.

I decided to check out the gaming stations next, but that's when I saw him: Thomas stood by the video-camera booth. He nodded along as the rep pointed and talked to him.

I was hoping for this, although it was odd that I had forgotten about him until this moment. I started this journey to get revenge, or to show that women could do as well or better than their male counterparts. But for some reason, I didn't feel like I had to prove anything now. I was purely happy to be here, whether he was here or not.

Suddenly he looked up and we locked eyes. He smiled, excused himself, and made his way over. I looked around for an excuse to escape, but it was too late.

"Hey, Jenna."

"Hi, Thomas," I replied cautiously.

"What are you doing here?"

"I'm competing in the tournament."

"Oh really? That's great."

I was listening for sarcasm or signs of criticism but heard none.

"I thought you didn't believe women could play video games. You made a big joke about it, remember?"

While I had let it go, I still never got to confront him about it. And now was the only chance I would have.

Thomas dropped his head then looked up. Was that shame on his face?

"I'm sorry about that, Jenna. Back in college, I was in a bad place. Some things had surfaced with my family. My mom had left when I was young. I was angry. Playing video games with my friends was always comforting growing up. When you came along, I liked you. But with gaming, I didn't know how to handle having a woman in my safe space, so I was an idiot and made that video as a joke. When really, the reason for doing it had little do with you."

"It was a terrible joke. But you also said other female gamers were gameplay trash."

Thomas's cheeks turned red. "I said that about everyone. But you're right, I was especially harsh on women back then."

"The video you posted and the jokes you made, they really affected my confidence." I didn't want to rehash the past or give him all the details, but he had to know that what he did had consequences.

"All I can say is that I'm sorry. It was stupid, and I know better now. I play online with all kinds of people now—equally." Thomas looked at me so intensely, I believed he was serious.

"Good. But why did you leave the video up?"

"Honestly, I forgot about it. I created a new account and started posting positive content. I haven't looked back."

"But you took it down recently."

His eyebrows drew together. "No, I didn't."

"Jenna!" someone called out.

I turned to see my teammates, TakeNote and Trekster. Take-note ran to me and pulled me into a hug while Trekster came up behind her. "Hey!" he said.

"Who's this?" Trekster asked, looking at Thomas.

"Oh, this is my ex, Thomas."

"The creator of *trained girl?*" he asked.

When I nodded, Trekster immediately stepped forward into Thomas's space. I put my hand on his shoulder, nudging him to take a step back.

"It's okay," I said. "It's water under the bridge." I turned to Thomas. "Look, I forgive you. Thank you for explaining everything, and I know this doesn't need to be said, but don't ever do that to anyone again."

"Thank you, and I won't. I've learned from my mistakes."

Trekster glared at Thomas for good measure. I guess he was less forgiving.

Thomas wandered off toward the games.

"Have you been here long?" TakeNote asked me.

I shook my head.

"Great, we can hang out before the tournament."

"I was about to check out the new games," I told them.

"Perfect," she said. "That's my favorite part." She laced her arm through mine, and we walked on, with Trekster trailing.

We three spent the next hour demoing games. I took note of a new platformer shooter game I was thinking about buying when it was released.

At the end of the game previews, I turned to my teammates. "I'm a bit nervous. I've never gamed in front of so many people before. It'll feel like I'm performing." It was the first time since my reveal that I felt like putting the mask on again. But those days were over; I had to stay strong. Not only for myself but for Eric.

"Nah," Trekster said. "Once you get your headset on, it'll be just like Button Mashers. You'll get into gameplay and tune out everything else."

The tournament today was a trio competition. Like at Button Mashers, players got points by the number of kills and end-game placement. Teams couldn't rely on placement alone. They would need to engage in fights to have enough points to win.

The DJ lowered his music, announced that the tournament would be starting soon, and asked competitors to report to their stations. The tournament would take place in an adjacent room and broadcast to the main room on the big screen for all to see.

"Well, I guess it's now or never," I said.

"Jenna, I have to tell you something," Trekster said. "I... won't be competing. At least not on your team."

"What? What do you mean? I thought the email said it would be the three of us. We all practiced together."

Trekster shuffled his feet. "Yeah, well, my replacement will be better."

"Better? What do you mean? I don't know—"

I was cut off when a familiar voice spoke my name.

I turned around to find Eric, standing with his hands in his pockets. He looked the same as he always had, but there was a brightness in his eyes I'd never seen before. He seemed happy. The underlying sadness was gone. I stared at him, thinking I was seeing a ghost.

"You'll be playing with EHucker," Trekster said behind me.

"You've *got* to be kidding me."

Chapter Thirty

ERIC

Not exactly the reaction I was hoping for. It wasn't like I expected her to run into my arms. Okay. Maybe I did. I at least thought she would be excited to see me.

She turned to Trekster with hands on hips. "What do you mean you're not going to be my partner? We practiced together almost every night last month."

I crossed my arms. Did they play games together every night? That explained why whenever I chatted with Trekster on the phone, he told me he had to go at eight. I had no right to be upset though. I asked for space, and I got it in spades. Though it about killed me. The few times I talked to Jenna, it pained me that I couldn't hold her. But I knew that if I returned too soon, I would fall back into pretending to be fine.

Trekster held up his hands in defense. "It'll be fine. I already discussed all our strategies with Eric. He's ready to go."

I couldn't see her face, but her shoulders moved up and down. I understood now. She wasn't angry at me, but she was anxious about the switch. I stepped forward and touched her shoulder.

"Jenna. Look at me."

She turned around and stared up at me with vulnerability in her eyes. "We got this. I promise."

Whatever she saw on my face, she must have decided she could trust me, because she nodded.

"I missed you," I whispered.

She was gorgeous in her dark jeans and a T-shirt that read *Can't Nerf This* with an MC Hammer character pictured below.

The reference made me smile. Her expression softened, and I wanted to pull her into my arms, but we were interrupted by a man in a Simmerz T-shirt.

"EHucker? I'm Malcolm. I'm one of the coordinators here at SimmerzCon. We're so glad you could join us. Everyone is excited you're here. Would you mind coming on stage this afternoon for a couple of the game presentations?"

I shifted uncomfortably on my feet. "Sorry, but no." I came to SimmerzCon for Jenna, and I wasn't ready to put myself on display for the whole Simmerz community.

"Don't worry, Malc. I'll do it." Trekster said, patting him on the back and nodding in my direction. He had my back.

An announcement rang out: "All competitors, please report to your stations and prepare for the first match!"

I followed Jenna and TakeNote to the numbered stations on their badges. I sat on her right while TakeNote took a seat to her left.

"Are you ready to give this a try?" I asked.

"No." She smiled. "I'm ready to win it all."

She turned back to her station to set up her headset and controller, and I did the same. We loaded into the lobby created for the competition.

The tournament was a total of six matches. To win, we would collectively have to score well by placing high and getting numerous kills.

In the first two games, we had some hiccups. We finished fourteenth in the first and were out of the second game quickly after we all died in the first few minutes. By the third game, we figured out our kinks and found our rhythm. We started scoring big points with many kills and high placements.

We were on our last game now and had to do well to win it all.

"That's it, TakeNote!" I said as she backtracked and took down a player who was chasing her.

"Three more to the west of us," said TakeNote.

"The east too," Jenna said.

"I see a truck. Hop in," I said.

"No, east is advancing on us. We're going to have to fight," Jenna replied.

"Grab the high ground," TakeNote said.

We fought the team advancing on us and got lucky when the team to the west decided to stay back. We were able to take the east team down, hop in the car, and move in with the circle. We found a buy station, where we were able to pick up necessary supplies.

"Extra shields," Jenna said, pinging what she dropped on the ground.

"Got it," I said.

As we advanced, we took out a couple more teams, and soon it would be down to four teams, then three, then two. We were on the edge of victory for the entire tournament in points. We needed this win.

But our position was not optimal; we were at the edge of a hill, and based on the position of the circle, the other team had the higher ground.

"I'm down!" TakeNote yelled.

"I'm on it." But before I could make a move, she was shot and eliminated.

"Two upper left, one right," Jenna said.

"I got right." I scaled the mountainside, luck on my side. The player made a mistake and peeked at the wrong time, so I was able to get a good angle and smoke him.

"Eric, watch out!" said Jenna.

I pivoted too late. The other two players noticed me and took me out. Jenna was now on her own.

"You got this, Jenson."

Her gamertag name just slipped out. I turned to see her tiny grin, but then it disappeared; she was concentrating again. All I could do was watch my screen, consumed in the action unfolding at a breakneck speed.

The final circle moved in her favor, toward lower ground. The other team would have to jump.

"Just like Button Mashers," she muttered.

I didn't know what she was referring to, but I could imagine she'd already faced this scenario a thousand times.

She attacked up the mountainside right before the circle changed, which forced a quick flight for both players. Crouching on a lower edge, she was able to shoot both players out of the air, and they fell to their deaths.

Credits rolled, and our animated characters entered the chopper, victorious. Cheers erupted from the main stage in the other room. Jenna jumped up, realizing what we did.

"We won!" she shouted, jumping up from her seat.

I stood and finally pulled her into my arms.

"We did."

A half hour later, everyone was in the main room, sitting before the stage for presentations for new games and the awards. After the competition, we were immediately ushered out and given instructions on what would happen next. And we were asked to sit up front. I got out of helping with the announcements of new games that were not even available to demo yet, but it never occurred to me that if we won, we'd still have to go on stage.

My leg bounced up and down until I felt a warm hand on my knee. I glanced at Jenna, and she leaned over and spoke in my ear, "It's okay. I'm here." Her smile took the edge off.

I tried to relax and focus on the new games, which Trekster was describing on stage, making it ten times more entertaining.

After the final game, he said, "Now that looks like something I'd want to try."

Caleb, the presenter, smiled and nodded along with him. "Okay Trekster, that's it for the new games. It's been a pleasure having you on stage. If you can, stick around for another minute because you know the next person coming up rather well. It's time for our award presentation!"

Trekster looked my way and gave me a thumbs-up, but his confidence appeared to wane for a moment. He seemed worried for me.

Caleb invited the second- and third-place teams up, to talk with the streamers and the invited competitor. My attention drifted until finally it was our turn.

"Next let's invite the winning team up: TakeNote, EHucker, and Jenna Hart!"

The audience applauded and cheered as we walked up the steps. Trekster greeted us on stage with hugs and handshakes. I faced the audience and cringed at all the phones facing us, either capturing a picture or recording. I focused on Caleb instead, who had begun interviewing TakeNote.

Breathe.

Remembering the exercises my therapist taught me, I breathed deeply, in and out. The anxiety slowly lifted.

I turned to Jenna, who was just staring at the audience, rooted on the spot. I internally kicked myself. This wasn't about me. This was her dream, and it was her first time being presented as a competitive gamer. She wasn't used to this level of attention.

I leaned over to whisper to Jenna, but Caleb turned in my direction.

"EHucker, I know everyone waited years to find out who you are. Finally your identity as Eric Slayter was revealed, but then you stopped streaming. Can you tell me how you reached that decision and what brought you back today?"

The room was silent. The audience, still holding up their phones, waited for answers. They deserved them. And I had prepared myself. I was ready.

Trekster stepped forward and cleared his throat, ready to help. I shook my head at him and brought the mic to my mouth. "Hello. Yes, I'm Eric Slayter, or you likely know me as EHucker. When I started streaming, I was coming off a career-ending injury in snowboarding. I didn't want to face people. I didn't even want to face myself. At least until recently, when I learned that strength is walking in the light and showing others who you really are. The reason I'm here is Jenna, someone with patience, courage, and determination. She's our true champion today."

Everyone cheered, and I passed the mic over to her. I bent down to whisper in her ear, "I see you." I saw her from the beginning, and I saw her now.

"Thank you for sharing, EHucker," said Caleb. "Now let's learn who our state victor is, though Eric gave you a great introduction already. Jenna, how did you prepare for SimmerzCon?"

Jenna spoke softly into the mic: "I spent many hours gaming with Trekster and TakeNote and competed in monthly tournaments at a local arcade bar called Button Mashers."

"You were set to compete with Trekster until today. How did you manage to adapt your strategy when told you'd be gaming with someone new?"

Jenna glanced at me. "Actually, I've gamed with EHucker before."

The audience broke out in whispers.

"Really?" said Caleb. "EHucker is private. How did that happen?"

"It's a long story, but I met Eric before I met EHucker. I didn't know it was him at first."

Now the room launched into chaos, with full-throated voices and clicking cameras. I didn't expect the questions to go this way, yet I wasn't surprised. Better to get it out now.

"I let a video of me hurt me, and it affected how I related to other gamers. I disguised myself as a guy because I didn't want anyone to recognize me, and I wanted to be judged on my skills alone. Eric convinced me that there are still good people out there, that it was safe to open up to them. He showed me the fun of gaming online again, and eventually I was no longer afraid. I showed up as myself and gained so much more than I ever had gaming under an alias.

"So you two are good friends?"

Jenna took my hand and faced me. "No, he is the man I love."

The audience gasped, but I barely heard them. I was done being apart from her. I would walk through this life with her, through the good and the bad. I would share my pain and my joy. She was it.

Caleb presented our award, and the four of us were soon led off the stage and into a back room.

"We can give you two a minute, but then we've got to bounce," Trekster said.

"Thank you," I replied.

Trekster and TakeNote slipped out and shut the door behind them.

"Jenna."

She closed the gap between us and pressed her lips to mine. When she pulled back, she smiled.

"I love you," I blurted out. "I've loved you for a while. I just couldn't say it. Not when I was in a bad place. You deserved better than that."

"Eric." She took my face in her hands so that all I saw was her. "I deserve *you.* I love you if you're happy and full of joy, and I love you if you're lost and struggling. Your heart is my heart, and I know how it feels because you saw me when I was lost. I understand why you had to take a step back, but even if you're still working on things, I can handle it. If you let me in, I will be here for you."

I pulled her close and kissed her forehead.

"You are everything I never knew I needed. You were my light when I was in the dark. You helped me feel again. Now I want to stand by your side, where we can brighten the world together. I will stay," I said, reiterating what she once promised me.

A tear slipped down Jenna's cheek as she smiled.

"Matt would have been so proud of you."

"I know," she whispered.

I leaned down and brought her lips to mine again.

Suddenly a voice broke the silence: "Uh, guys?" And we pulled back.

Trekster stood there smiling with his arm wrapped around a woman I hadn't seen before. Tara, no doubt. TakeNote was there too.

"Coast is clear," he said. "There's an arcade bar up the street if you want to go. It's no Button Mashers, but..."

Jenna smiled at me mischievously. "A *Space Invader* rematch is calling our names."

"What's your bet?"

"Nothing." She stared into my eyes. "I've already won."

Chapter Thirty-One

ERIC

Three Months Later

"That's it for today. Remember chat, keep grinding."

Jenna removed her headset at the desk across from me. We were able to shove a second desk in my office so that we sat across from each other when we played online. Jenna started streaming with me every once in a while. We just finished a short stream for the morning. We both used a face cam. She clicked her mouse a few times. "Do you think we could find a better catchphrase?"

"And change what our community knows and loves? No way."

She rolled her eyes, then got up and turned toward the door. But I grabbed her arm and pulled her onto my lap.

"Hey!"

I nuzzled her neck.

"I love you," I mumbled.

She pulled back to look at me. "Are you doing okay?"

"I'm good. Just let me hold you."

She leaned back into my arms and ran her hands through my now short hair—it was one of the changes I needed to stay in the light. My scar would always be there, and now that the world knew, I didn't have to hide it.

A month after SimmerzCon, I returned to two things: school and my stream—studying to be a physical therapist while streaming on the side. Something I never gave up on when I was recuperating was the possibility of reaching my body's full potential. And though I couldn't snowboard anymore, I loved how far I had come and wanted to help others maximize their recovery too.

I missed my streaming community, and once the excitement died down, I saw that my chat did not care about my past. They just wanted to be social again, to interact. Making Jenna a part of that was just a natural extension. People seemed to love her as much, if not more than I did. And after our victory at SimmerzCon, everyone was intrigued.

While I enjoyed streaming, I made sure to keep it in perspective so that I could manage my anxiety. Some days I liked to hold Jenna when I was feeling anxious. Today was one of those days.

I pulled back from our hug and kissed her on the nose. "Ready to go to Button Mashers?"

"Yup. Let me get changed."

She hopped up and ran to the bedroom. I stretched and then stepped out onto the balcony, barefoot.

"Ow!" I jumped back and forth on the hot ground.

My phone rang, and I answered immediately.

"Hey man, what's up?" said Justin. "Great stream."

"You saw that?"

"Of course. But I have to say, you better be careful."

My stomach dropped. "Why?"

"Jenna's going to steal all your viewers."

I laughed. "That's fine. I would love that."

"Actually, I wanted to let you know I'll be in town for a couple of weeks next month."

"Really?"

"Yeah. It's a break in the season. I'd like to spend time with you if you're free. And then at the end of the summer, I'm helping Emily move."

"You are?"

Emily got accepted to a college in Colorado. I was a little sad and, honestly, surprised; I moved to the Midwest to be near my family and now she was moving back. I didn't understand why. Did she miss it there?

"Yeah, I'll fly in then drive her car out here so she doesn't have to go alone."

"Why isn't my dad taking her?"

"Because of that work conference. Remember?"

"Right."

Now that he mentioned it, I remembered Dad saying that he was going to attend a leadership conference that would give him lots of networking opportunities. His background as my coach gave him a lot of valuable experience, but he was also trying to learn more so that he could grow in his company.

"Well, I've got to go," Justin said. "See you soon."

I touched the *End* button and headed back inside. Jenna was ready in her dark jeans and a purple silk blouse that hugged her in all the right places.

"You look beautiful."

Her mouth spread into a slow smile. "Thanks. Let's go."

Chapter Thirty-Two

JENNA

"You got this, Henry. Look to your right… Yes, see that revive? Pick it up. He's going to be coming after you. Try to find positioning… Good. He doesn't see you. Wait until he's a little closer… Good. Now!"

Henry released a stream of bullets at the final player in the match, who was caught off guard, and he easily eliminated him.

"I won!" He jumped up from his chair and high-fived me.

"You didn't even need me. You did it on your own."

"Thanks though. Your coaching has really helped me be competitive."

"Anytime. I'll see you next week at the tournament."

After SimmerzCon, I was offered a coding job in a small gaming company, so I quit the café. Besides Henry, I started coaching some others who wanted to get better in the Button Masher tournament, as a way to still be involved there.

Walking toward Eric at the bar, I passed Carter, who nodded at me. We'd reached a point where we acknowledged each other but didn't engage beyond that.

I wrapped my arms around Eric. "Having fun?"

"I am. But even more so now." He leaned down to kiss me on the lips.

"Bleh!" Lewis made a gagging gesture and smiled.

"Knock it off. You know next time you see Ella you'll go all googly-eyed," I said.

"Yeah, if only she would show up," Lewis said.

Unfortunately, Ella hadn't been back since the last tournament.

Lewis acted like it didn't bother him, but I saw his eyes flick to the entrance each time the door opened.

"Come on," I said, pulling Eric toward the arcade.

"Coaching is going well?"

"Yeah, I really love it. I miss competing, but helping is fun too. So what did you want to do tonight?"

Eric rubbed his chin. "How about we play a classic?"

"Aren't they all classic?"

"Yes, but let's play *Space Invaders*. And let's make it interesting."

"What do you bet?"

"My heart." Eric dropped to one knee and pulled out a small box, then opened it to present a beautiful diamond ring with three round stones, the middle being the biggest and sparkling against the lights.

I gasped. In the corner stood Lewis, Bryan, and Alyssa, who had her phone up recording the whole thing.

"A person in the dark doesn't know he's lost until there's light. You are my light. My star in the night. A place I can always find to return home to. I love you, Jenna. Will you marry me?"

Tears fell down my cheek, and I nodded. "Yes! I will marry you!"

Eric slid the ring onto my finger, and our friends swarmed around us, congratulating us and exchanging hugs. But the room faded away as Eric pressed his forehead to mine.

"I see you," he said.

"And I see you," I replied.

We saw in each other the versions of ourselves we tried to hide from the world. Not Jenson. Not EHucker. We saw the people we were meant to be.

"About that match..." I said.

We stepped up to *Space Invaders* and took our spots.

"No funny business," he muttered.

"You mean like this?" I teased while squeezing his bicep.

Before I could turn to the screen, Eric leaned down and pressed his lips to mine once more. When he pulled back, I stared into his eyes.

"You mean funny business like that?" he said.

I laughed, turned to the screen, and pressed *Start*.

Acknowledgments

When I first started writing this story, I was coming out of a difficult season in my life and was new to the world of online gaming and streaming. I started dreaming about a story with characters in the online gaming world that had real struggles and hope to overcome them. As I grew in my writing and experience in gaming, my story and characters grew with me. I'm excited to finally bring my characters to life and I hope that whether someone is a gamer or not, that they enjoy the Button Masher world.

There are many people to thank for the help and support as I wrote this book. To my beta readers who read the early rough drafts, Kevin, Emily, Michelle, Carrie, Althea, and Jason. Thank you for believing and encouraging me in the earliest part of my story.

Thank you to Bob Goff's writing class that helped me get started. Thank you to the Hope Writers Community. I've met some wonderful people and learned a lot from that community. And to the Typewriter Creative Co. that helped me bring my book to the finish line.

I want to especially thank Michelle who I met in a Hope Circle. Thank you for keeping in touch and cheering me on until the end. It has made the world of difference to have a writing friend come alongside me on this journey.

Thank you to my editors Sara and Lisa. Sara helped me refine the connections of my characters and make them the best versions of themselves. Lisa saw the parts of my writing that I couldn't fix on my own and really refined my story into its best version. Thank you to my final proofreader, Lee Ann, who gave my story a final read-through.

To my gaming friends who showed me how wonderful online friendships and communities can be. Thank you to Luke, Colin, Scott, Tony, Taylor, and all the sweet friends in those communities. Also thank you to Jon and Liz who inspired me by how they genuinely care for and foster kind, growing communities online. And to all my new gaming friends that I have met in the past year. Thank you for your encouragement, support, and friendships.

A special thank you to my friends and family. To all the people that I have told, "I'm writing a book," and have followed along and listened to me progress along the way to the very end.

Finally, thank you to Jason, my husband, and biggest supporter in the world. You believed in me from first draft to the final product. You encouraged me through all my doubts, listened to me read through multiple rewrites, and never let me give up.

About the Author

Katelyn Hook writes clean contemporary romances with heart. She loves stories with redemption, love, and hope. When she doesn't have a book in hand, she can be found gaming online with friends or watching an anime with her husband. *Button Mashers* is her debut novel.

CONNECT WITH KATELYN

www.katelynhook.com
www.instagram.com/katelynhookwriter/
www.facebook.com/katelynhookwriter/